T0348115

To Ruby,
the best donkey of all

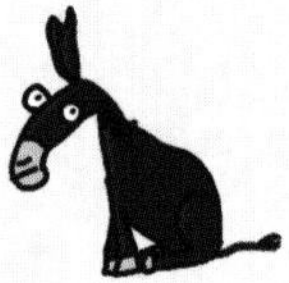

First Dog On The Moon presents

The story of

The Christmas Story

by
Andrew Marlton

Text Publishing Melbourne Australia

The Text Publishing Company

Swann House
22 William Street
Melbourne Victoria 3000
Australia
textpublishing.com.au

First published in 2010 by The Text Publishing Company
Printed in China by Everbest Printing Co Ltd

National Library of Australia
Cataloguing-in-Publication entry
Marlton, Andrew.
First Dog on the Moon Christmas story / Andrew Marlton.
1st ed.
ISBN: 9781921656750 (pbk.)
Christmas–Humor. Christmas stories.
A823.4

Introduction!

Welcome, gentle reader, to our little book of Christmas marvellousness.

Christmas, as you know, is a time of thoughtful sharing and eating yummy things. A time for giving thanks and reflecting on the good fortune we may have. You are lucky enough to be reading this extremely beautiful book, so you can certainly take a moment to be grateful for that!

I would just like to thank myself for reading this book to me

Dearly beloved, you hold in your tiny Christmassy paws the wondrous tale of the Christmas Story. A tale that humans have delighted in telling, every Christmas, for ever so long.

Your tiny Christmassy paws are...

here

and here

But do you know where the story of the Christmas Story comes from?

No, Yes, Sort of

It's in 𝕿𝖍𝖊 𝕭𝖎𝖇𝖑𝖊!

You may have heard of **𝕿𝖍𝖊 𝕭𝖎𝖇𝖑𝖊**. It's a fat book full of stories, written down long ago by lots of different people for lots of different reasons. We won't go into all of that.

The important thing to know is that the Christmas Story first appears in two particular bits of **𝕿𝖍𝖊 𝕭𝖎𝖇𝖑𝖊**:

𝕿𝖍𝖊 𝕲𝖔𝖘𝖕𝖊𝖑 𝕬𝖈𝖈𝖔𝖗𝖉𝖎𝖓𝖌 𝖙𝖔 𝕸𝖆𝖙𝖙𝖍𝖊𝖜 and 𝕿𝖍𝖊 𝕲𝖔𝖘𝖕𝖊𝖑 𝕬𝖈𝖈𝖔𝖗𝖉𝖎𝖓𝖌 𝖙𝖔 𝕷𝖚𝖐𝖊.

This is the Bible

This bit isn't very Christmassy, it just looks like Jesus is having a nice bath.

The Bible contains some of the Christmas Story but not the whole thing and even those bits are sort of confusing!

Don't touch it! It looks old!

Really?

This, oh my tiny tinkly Christmas bell, is where the story begins.

Or actually, where the stories begin – because **𝕸𝖆𝖙𝖙𝖍𝖊𝖜** and **𝕷𝖚𝖐𝖊** don't always agree on exactly what happened.

But more about that later...

In the meantime, just to make it more confusing...

Even **The Bible** isn't the whole story of the story. True!

Some parts of this stupendous tale have just wandered in by themselves over time, popping up all over the place. Like a dear friend, dropping in now and then for a cup of tea and a chat, and wondering if you might have any of those little cheesy biscuits you sometimes make.

I thought I'd drop in and say hello to your biscuits
I'll just put the kettle on

Oh my little lost festive sock, how shall we find our way through the terrible maze of Christmas?

This way to the occasionally dangerous Land Of Christmas
Feral Christmas Puddings
Marauding candy canes
Angry mince pies disguised as little elves
Whadda you looking at?
Nobody here but us elfs

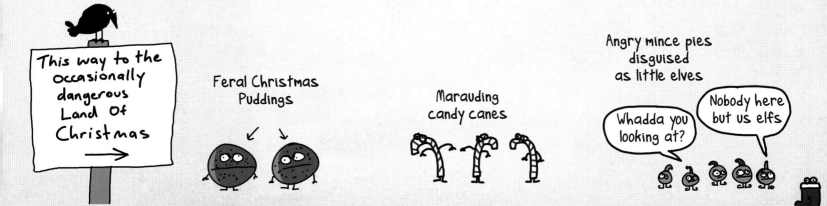

Easy. We just need a few wise and steadfast companions.

Ooh look, here they are now!

The brave and sturdy beast who does most of the hard work in the Christmas Story.

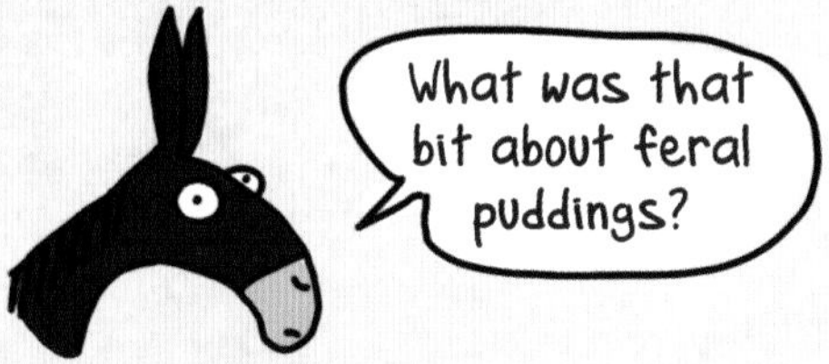
What was that bit about feral puddings?

To solve ancient Christmas mysteries and explain the historical bits and pieces, we have a team of erudite biblical scholars!

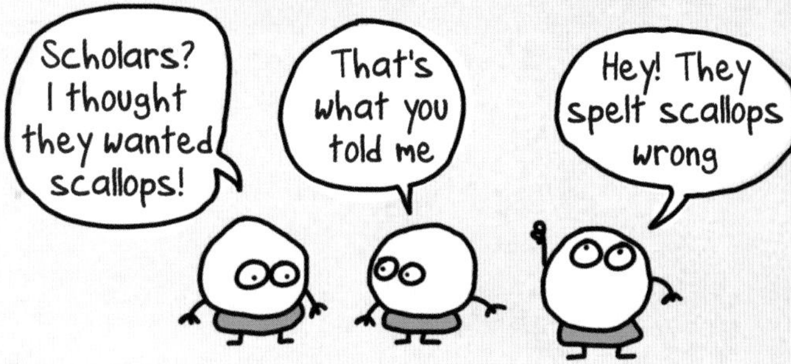
Scholars? I thought they wanted scallops!
That's what you told me
Hey! They spelt scallops wrong

Finally, a cornucopia of angels, beetles, chocolate biscuits, Christmas ants and other mysterious yuletide beasties.

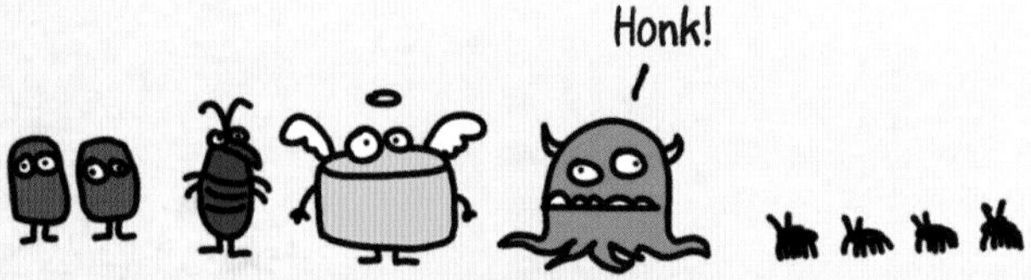
Honk!

Important Note: The person who really does most of the work is Mary because she has to give birth to an actual baby, but more of that later.

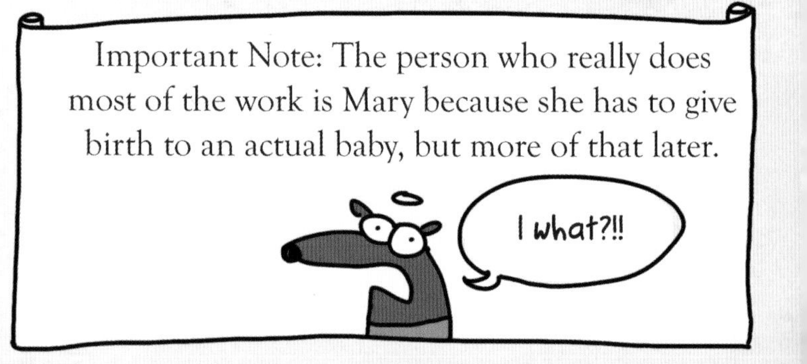
I what?!!

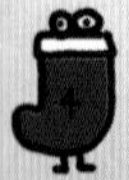

Now you must listen carefully, my crunchy little Christmas biscuit, for we are about to begin our most excellent tale.

The Christmas Story starts before Jesus was born, and it starts with a woman called Mary.

We don't know much about Mary, but that hasn't stopped people painting a lot of pictures of her:

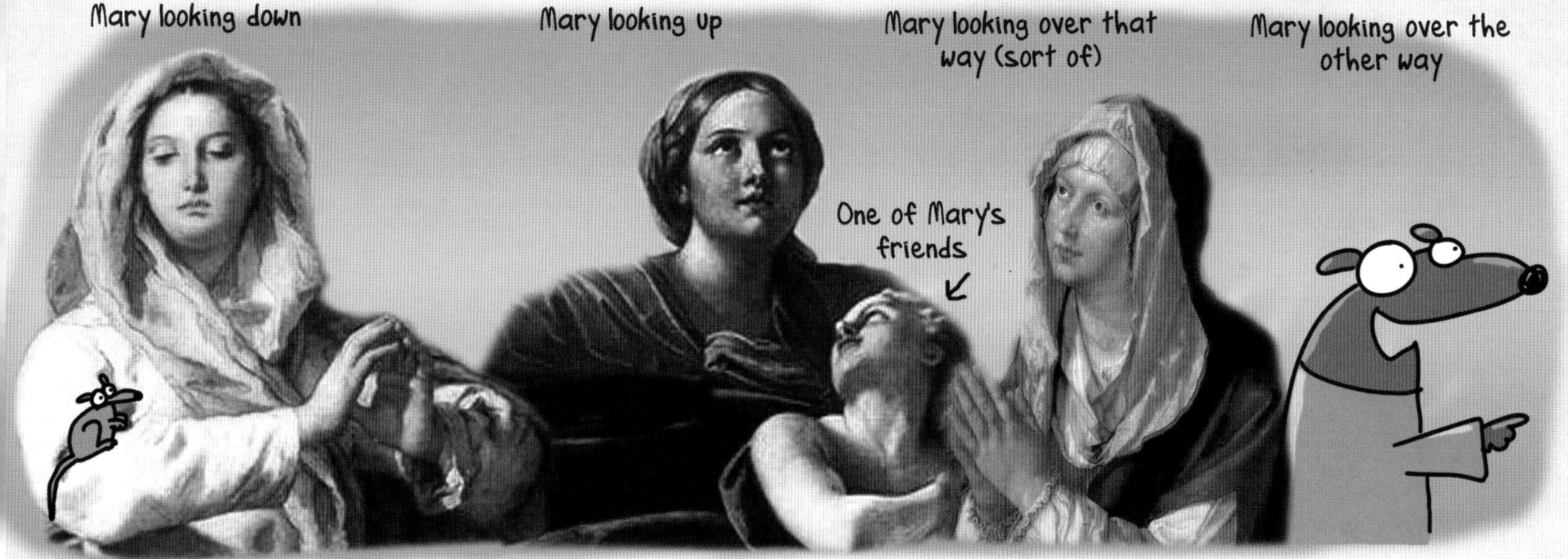
Mary looking down
Mary looking up
Mary looking over that way (sort of)
Mary looking over the other way
One of Mary's friends

We are told she was a virgin, which means she hadn't done any of the things you have to do to have a baby.

And that, oh my crisp and delicious fruit flan, is why people get so excited about the whole 'Mary having a baby' story.

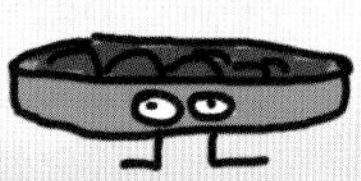
crisp and delicious

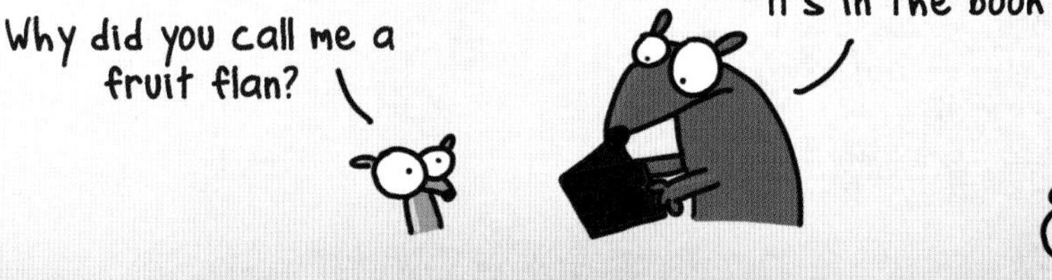
Why did you call me a fruit flan?
It wasn't me! It's in the book

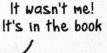

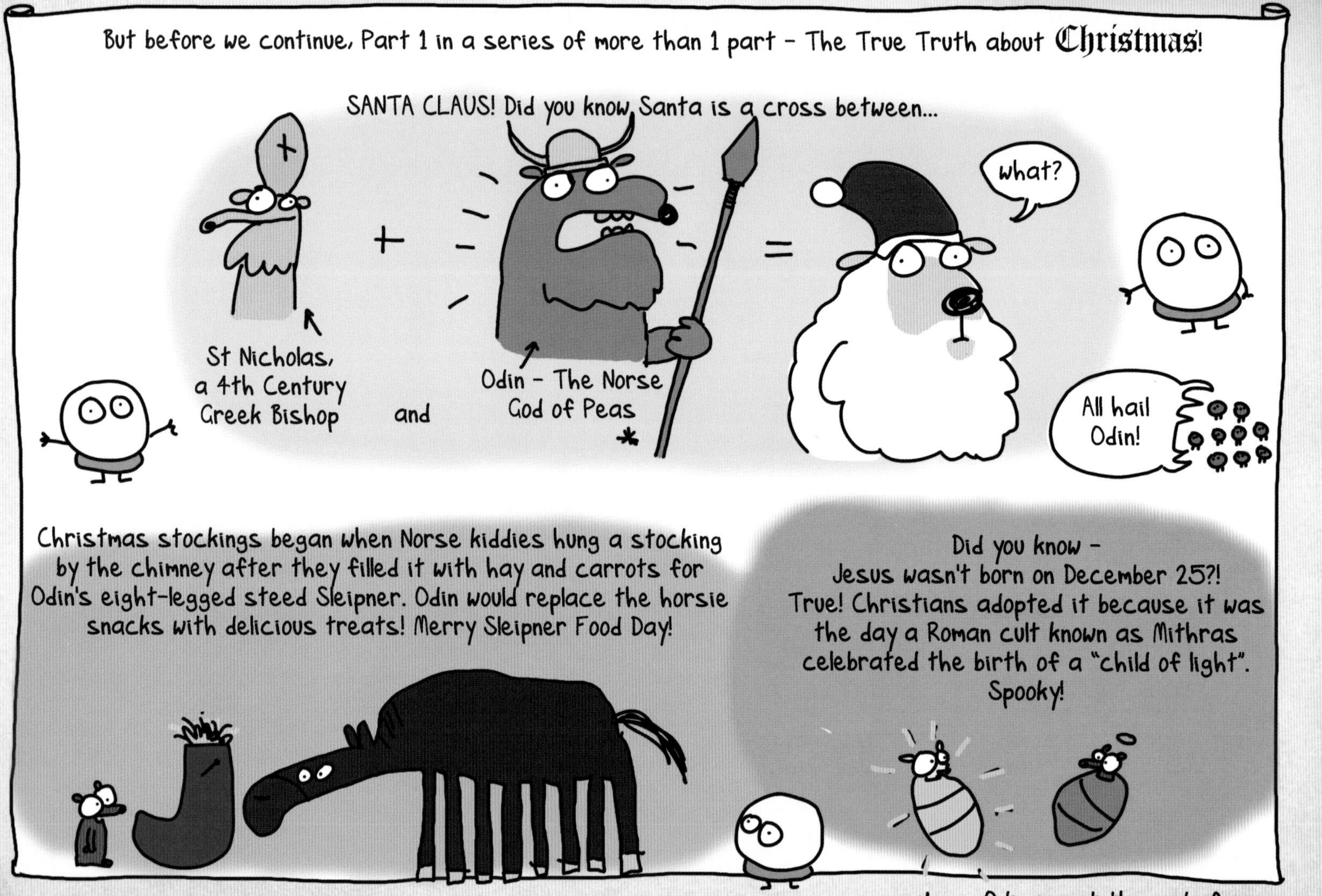
But before we continue, Part 1 in a series of more than 1 part – The True Truth about Christmas!
SANTA CLAUS! Did you know, Santa is a cross between...
St Nicholas, a 4th Century Greek Bishop
and
Odin – The Norse God of Peas *
what?
All hail Odin!
Christmas stockings began when Norse kiddies hung a stocking by the chimney after they filled it with hay and carrots for Odin's eight-legged steed Sleipner. Odin would replace the horsie snacks with delicious treats! Merry Sleipner Food Day!
Did you know – Jesus wasn't born on December 25?! True! Christians adopted it because it was the day a Roman cult known as Mithras celebrated the birth of a "child of light". Spooky!

* Odin is not the god of peas

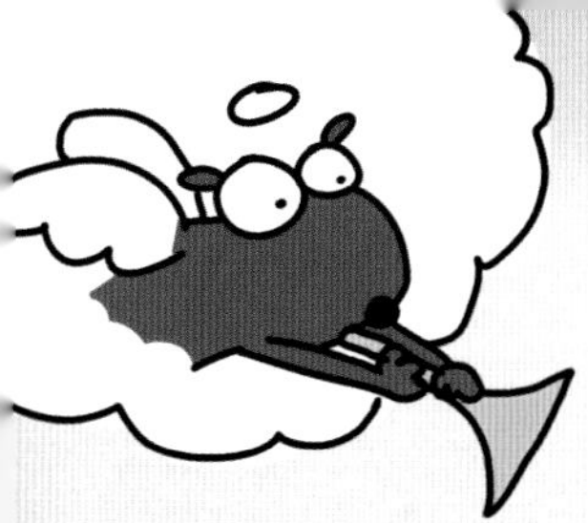

It all started when **God** sent an angel to talk to Mary...

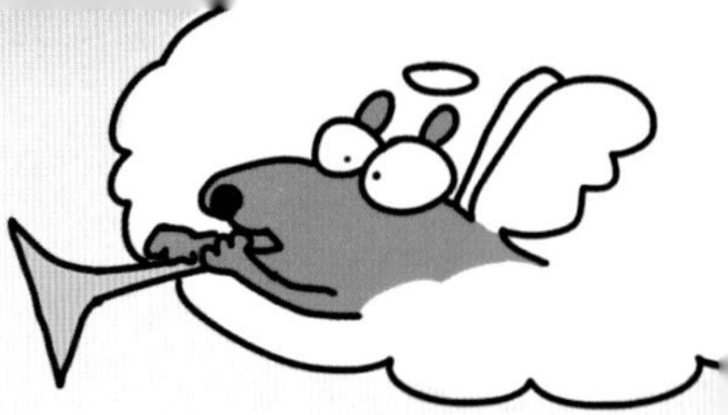

The Annunciation

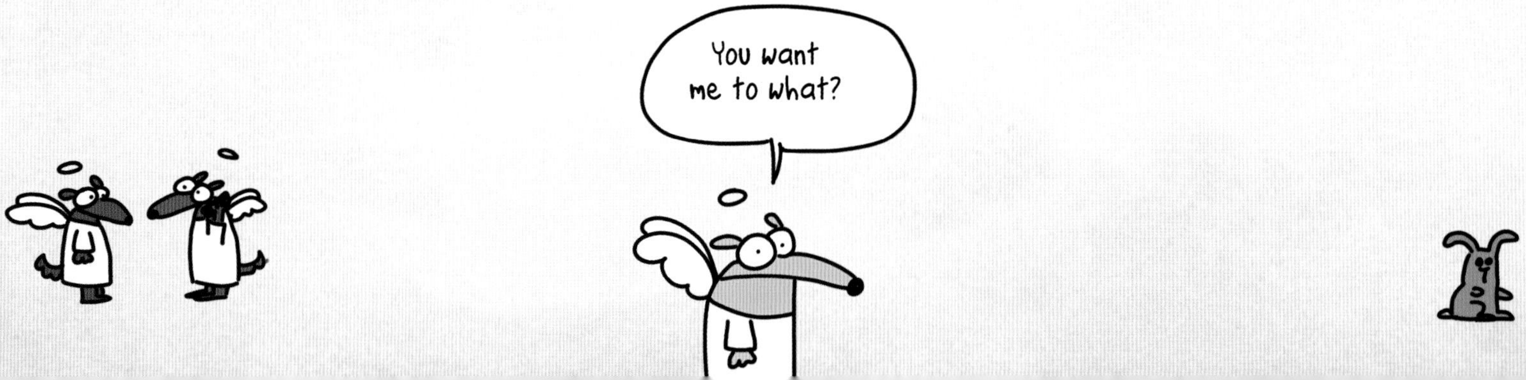
You want me to what?

Time for the next part in our gripping series of Handy Christmas Facts: The true truth about Angels

Angels in the Christmas Story are always shown in human form. Because they are supposed to have great power, the could probably have taken any form they felt like! For example:

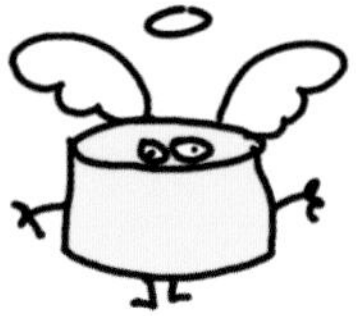

cheese

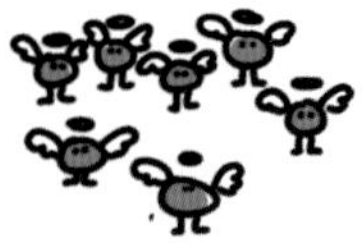

peas

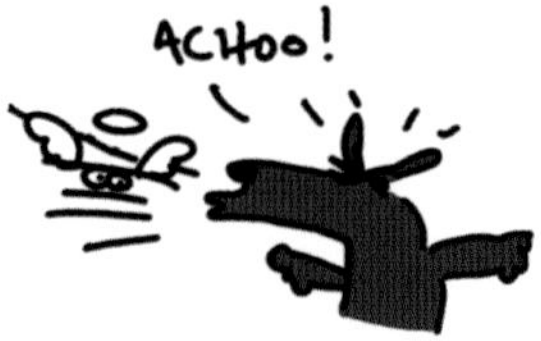
ACHOO!

a sneeze

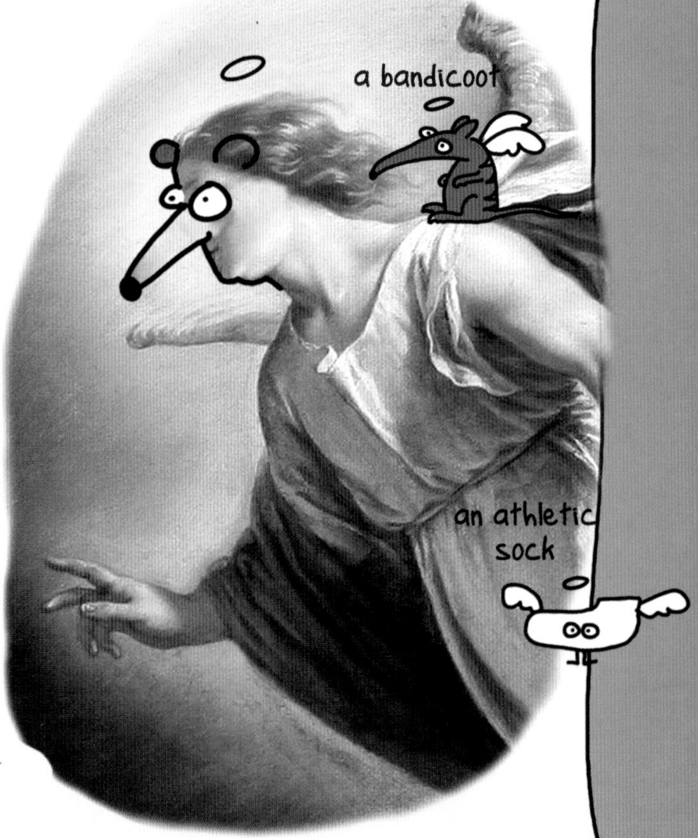
a bandicoot
an athletic sock

For the purposes of our story, we will portray angels in human form as shown here

like this

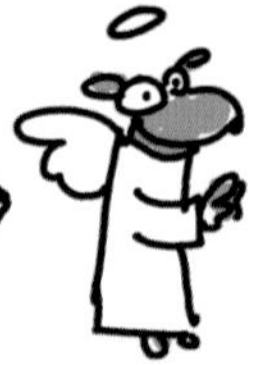

with robes

and this

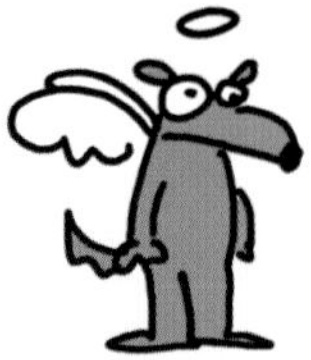

without robes

You may have heard mention, oh my tiny baby reindeer, of someone called **God**.
People don't often agree on quite who or what **God** is, but in our story **God** looks like this:

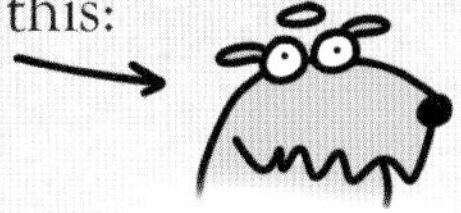

Now, one particular day in June some time past, **God** was in Heaven,
having a chat with an angel.
'Gabriel,' said **God** (because that was the angel's name) 'I want you to go to Nazareth and talk to a very nice young virgin called Mary. She's going to have a baby and call him Jesus.
Can you let her know please?'
'How unusual,' said Gabriel. 'I'll go and tell her right away.'

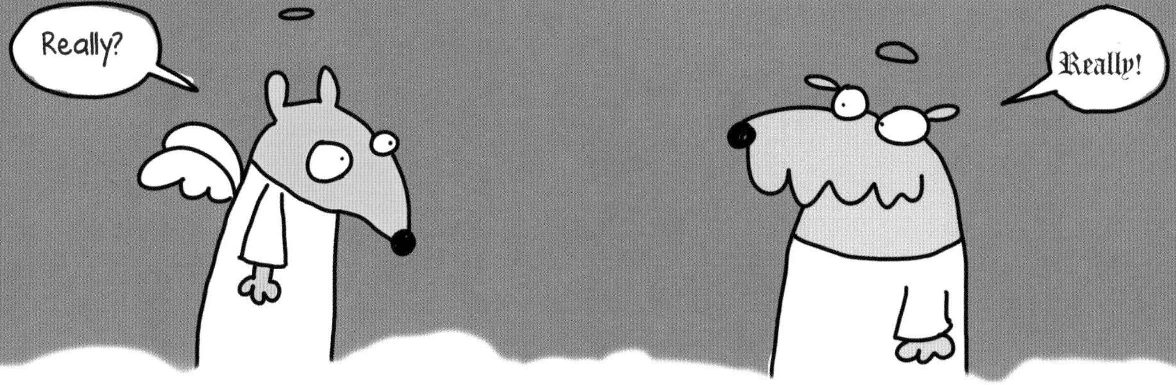
Really?
Really!

Now it so happened

that Mary was engaged to be married to a man named
Joseph, by all accounts a lovely fellow.

But Joseph was
down at the shop when
Gabriel came round. And so
Mary found herself face to face with a strange angel. Right there in her own kitchen!

'Who art thou?' Mary shrieked.

'Relax!' said Gabriel, 'Thou art highly favoured with the Lord.'

'Really?' said Mary. 'Well I never.'

'I know,' said Gabriel. 'And plus, thou art going to have a baby and thou shalt call his name Jesus!'

rock on!

Oh my teeny spore of endangered fungus,

according to

The Gospel of Luke,

Mary was agog!

'How shall this be,' she said to Gabriel, 'seeing I know not a man?'
(Or in other words she was a virgin, as previously discussed.)

And Gabriel said, 'Because **God** can really do pretty much anything he wants to,
that's just how the whole **God** thing seems to work.'

What?

Is this some
kind of joke?

Get out of here
you big flying weirdy!

How shall
this be?

Did you know "agog" is not a goth frog? True!

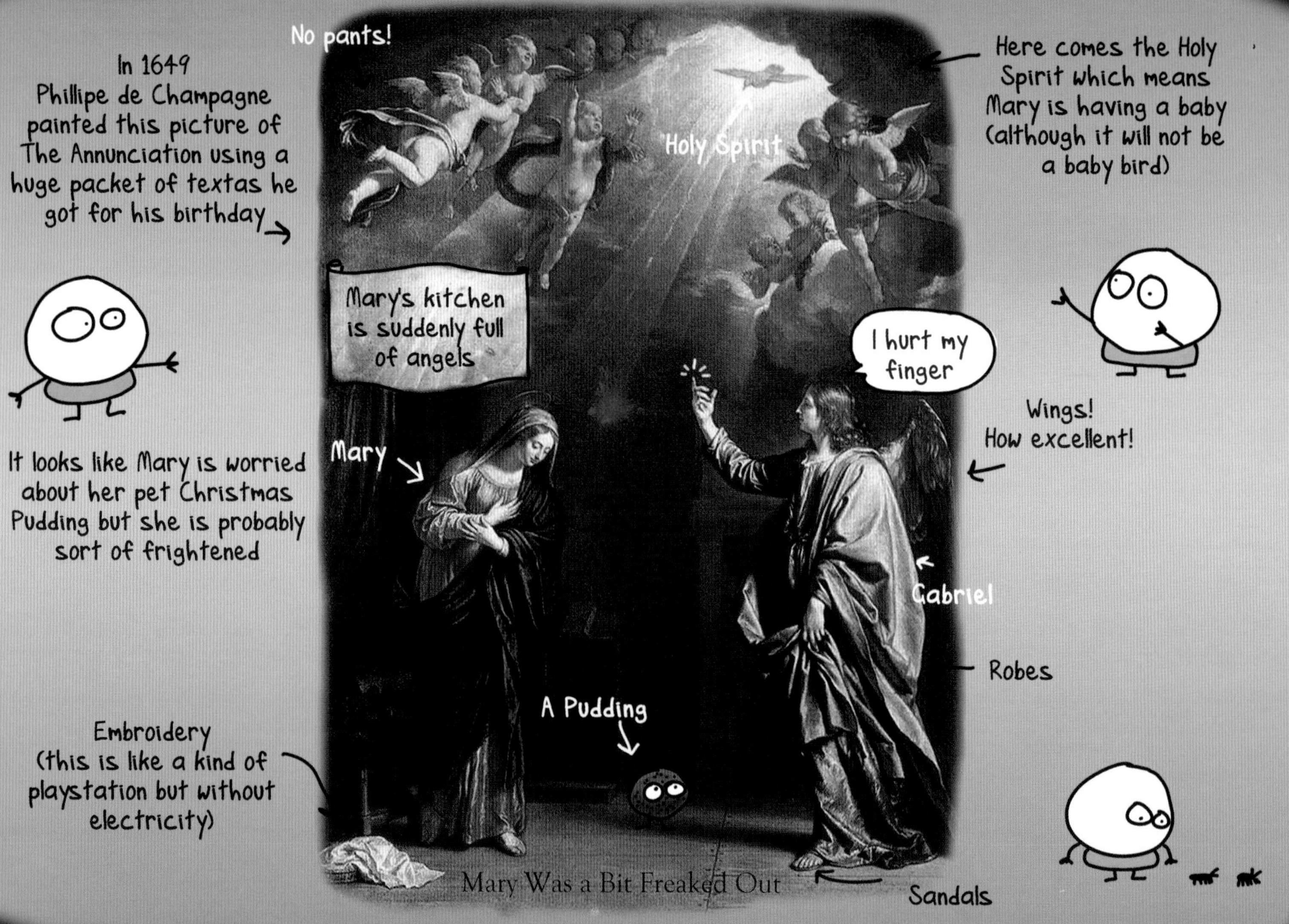

In 1649 Phillipe de Champagne painted this picture of The Annunciation using a huge packet of textas he got for his birthday
No pants!
Holy Spirit
Here comes the Holy Spirit which means Mary is having a baby (although it will not be a baby bird)
Mary's kitchen is suddenly full of angels
I hurt my finger
Wings! How excellent!
Mary
It looks like Mary is worried about her pet Christmas Pudding but she is probably sort of frightened
Gabriel
Robes
A Pudding
Embroidery (this is like a kind of playstation but without electricity)
Sandals

Mary Was a Bit Freaked Out

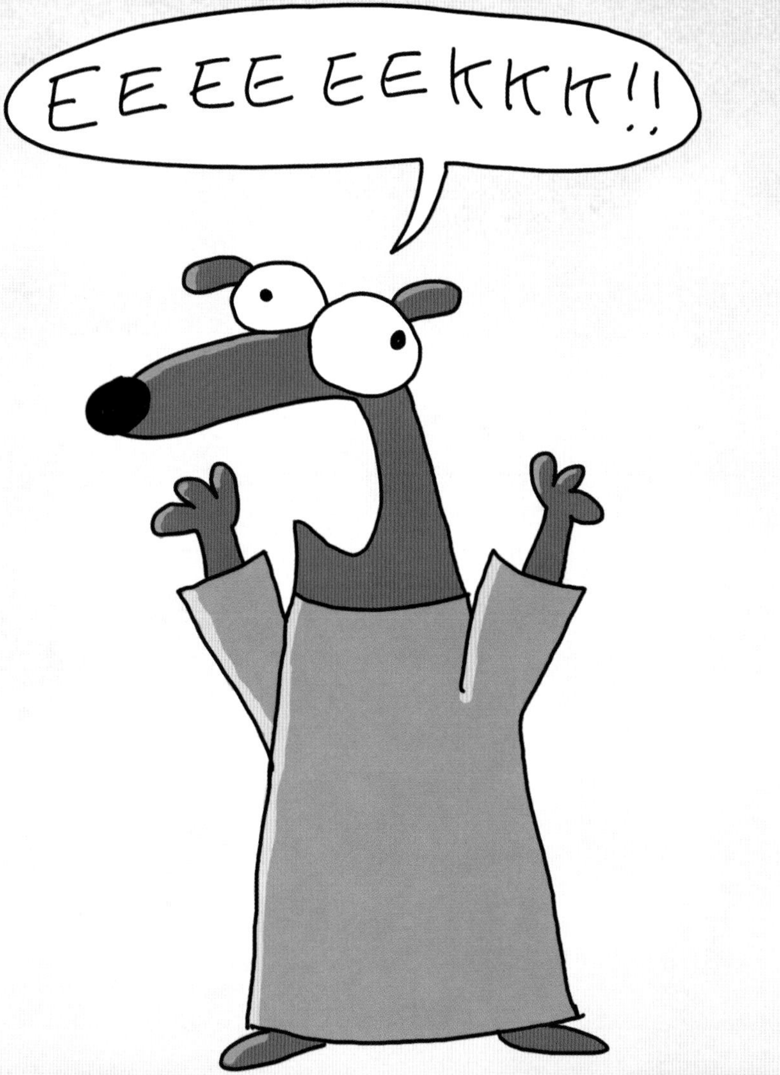
EEEEEEKKK!!

Eventually Mary calmed down and Gabriel told her some other news.

'You know your cousin Elizabeth?' he said. 'The really old one? Far too old to have a baby?'

'What about her?' said Mary.

'She's going to have a baby!' yelled Gabriel. '𝕳𝖔𝖙 𝕯𝖎𝖌𝖌𝖊𝖙𝖞! It's 𝕲𝖔𝖉 again – another miracle!'

So listen carefully, my little electric croquembouche.

Mary went to visit Elizabeth.

She was probably thinking they would have quite a bit to talk about.

The Visitation

NAZARETH
HILL COUNTRY

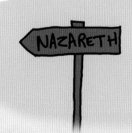

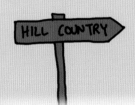

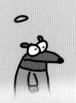

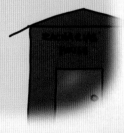

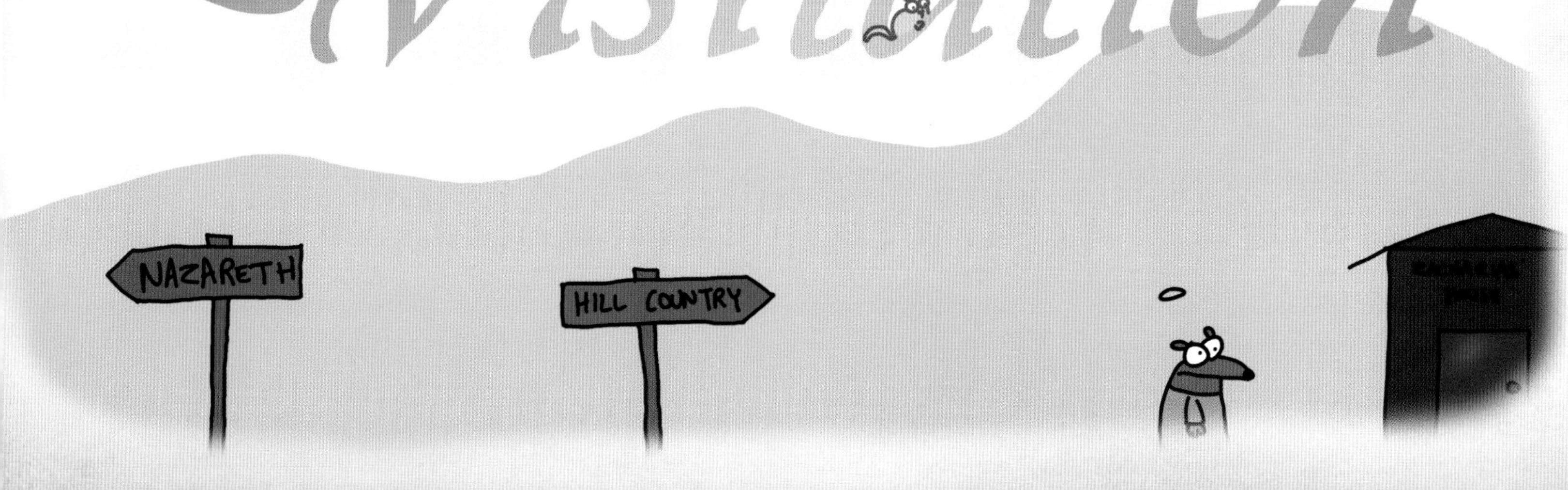

Mary knocked on the door and said hello how are you dear and *at that very moment* Elizabeth suddenly felt her baby moving inside her. She really was pregnant like the Angel Gabriel said! Even though it was impossible!

Boinnngg!

Probably what Mary said then is, do you have any ice cream no wait I feel like watermelon and sardines, and after lunch she sang a song about God. But you can't hear it because this is a book and not a musical, you will just have to imagine it.

Joy to the world, the Lord is come etc.
Do you know Rudolph the Red Nosed Reindeer?
ICE CREAM
POTATO CHIPS

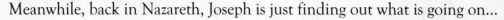

Meanwhile, back in Nazareth, Joseph is just finding out what is going on...

There is no official name for this bit so we shall just call it...

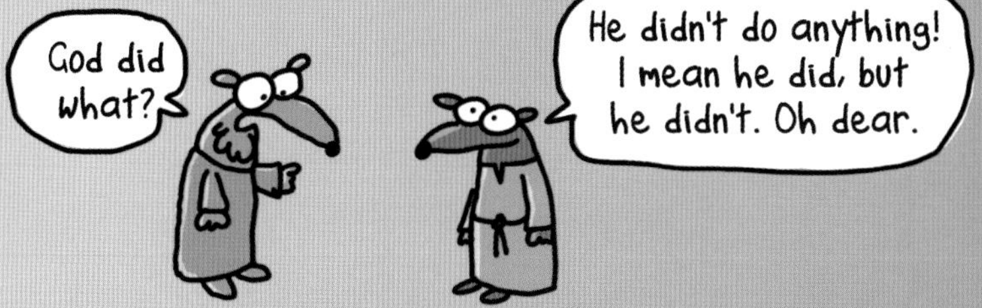
God did what?
He didn't do anything! I mean he did, but he didn't. Oh dear.

Joseph's bit of the story

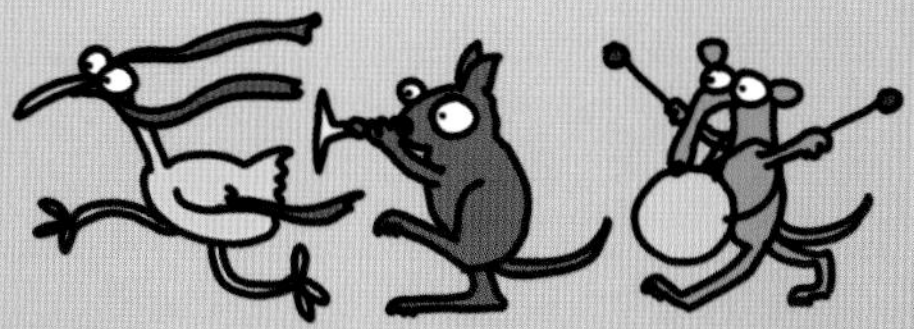

I must tell you, oh my sparkly bit of tinsel, that when Joseph
learned about all this he thought very seriously about calling the wedding off.

'Not only is Mary having someone else's baby,' Joseph muttered to himself,
'she says it's 𝕲𝖔𝖉 who is the father. I mean, I beg your pardon?'

He was probably sad and most likely a bit cross. Even a lot cross.

sad
Joseph

angry
Joseph

distracted
by a birdie
Joseph

Then Joseph had a dream about an angel. The angel told him it was all a glorious, crisp and glittering miracle that 𝔊𝔬𝔡 had chosen him to be one of the dads of Jesus. 'Rejoice!' said the angel 'and be chuffed. It is Christmas after all.' And when he awoke, Joseph did just that.

You left your lights on

Oh my demented piece of fluff, in those days when our story takes place, women and girls had a difficult time. They were seen as belonging to men, like cows and sheep and toasters. How rude! And if you were pregnant like Mary and you didn't have a husband, you were in big trouble.

I think I'm pregnant

Baaa?

Now, back to the **Gospels of Matthew and Luke.**

(You remember, the jolly fellows who first wrote the Christmas Story?)

Matthew lived in Galilee. He was a tax collector so he was quite unpopular. He actually knew Jesus – he invited him over for dinner one time and Jesus went because that was just the kind of fellow he was.

Would you like another chocolate biscuit Jesus?
I mustn't, I'm absolutely stuffed

This is Rembrandt's painting of Matthew and the Angel →

Matthew is the one with the beard

Some of Matthew's other little friends

Important Historical Note :
It was a time of beards.
There were beards, beards everywhere!

It turns out Matthew didn't actually write **The Gospel of Matthew.**

It was some other guy and nobody knows who.

I thought you knew
Me? No she does
I don't think it was me

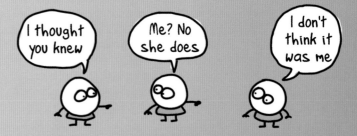

Luke, on the other hand, did write **The Gospel of Luke**. He was a Greek doctor and a historian-writing sort of fellow. He lived when Jesus was alive but, unlike Matthew, he never met him.

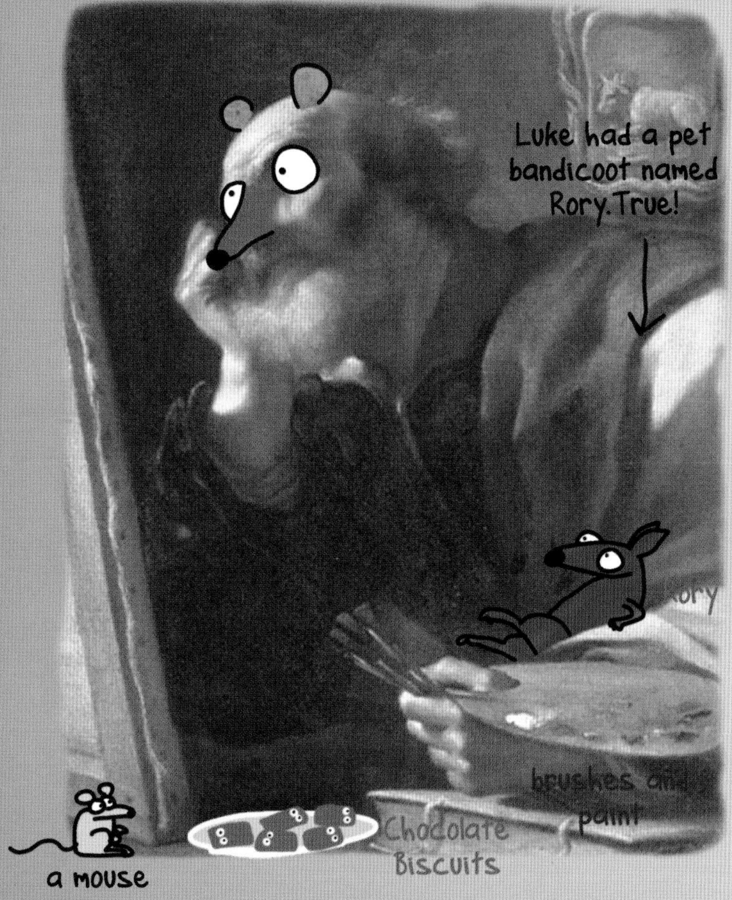

Luke had a pet bandicoot named Rory. True!
brushes and paint
Chocolate Biscuits
a mouse

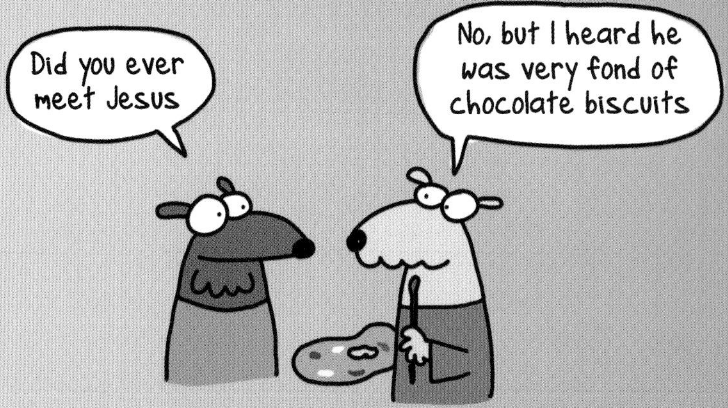

Did you ever meet Jesus
No, but I heard he was very fond of chocolate biscuits

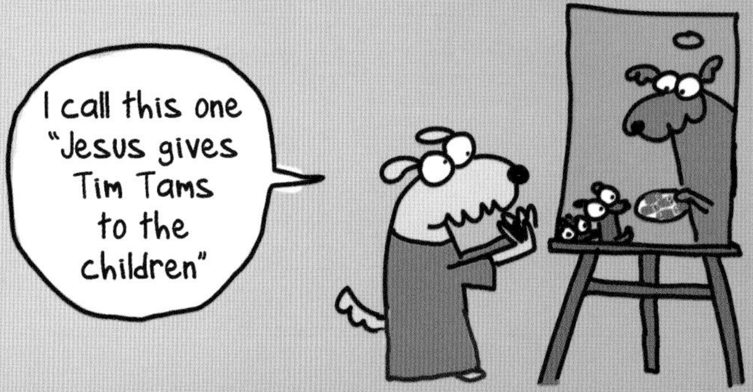

I call this one "Jesus gives Tim Tams to the children"

Now my angry little mince pie, on with the story...

Luke says: *And it came to pass that a decree went out that all the world should be registered.*

This means the emperor Caesar Augustus wanted everyone to

Register for Reasons Related to Taxation (which is not even slightly Christmassy).

So all went to be registered, everyone to his own city.

Joseph's city was Bethlehem, where his family came from.

Mary had to go there with him because she was ~~a toaster~~ his fiancée.

Here is where Matthew disagrees with Luke.

Matthew says Joseph and Mary already lived in Bethlehem.

That would make the Christmas Story a bit dull though.

Aloha!

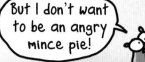

"Joseph and Mary travelled to the lounge room but there was no room on the couch because there was a cow sitting there"

But I don't want to be an angry mince pie!

The Nativity

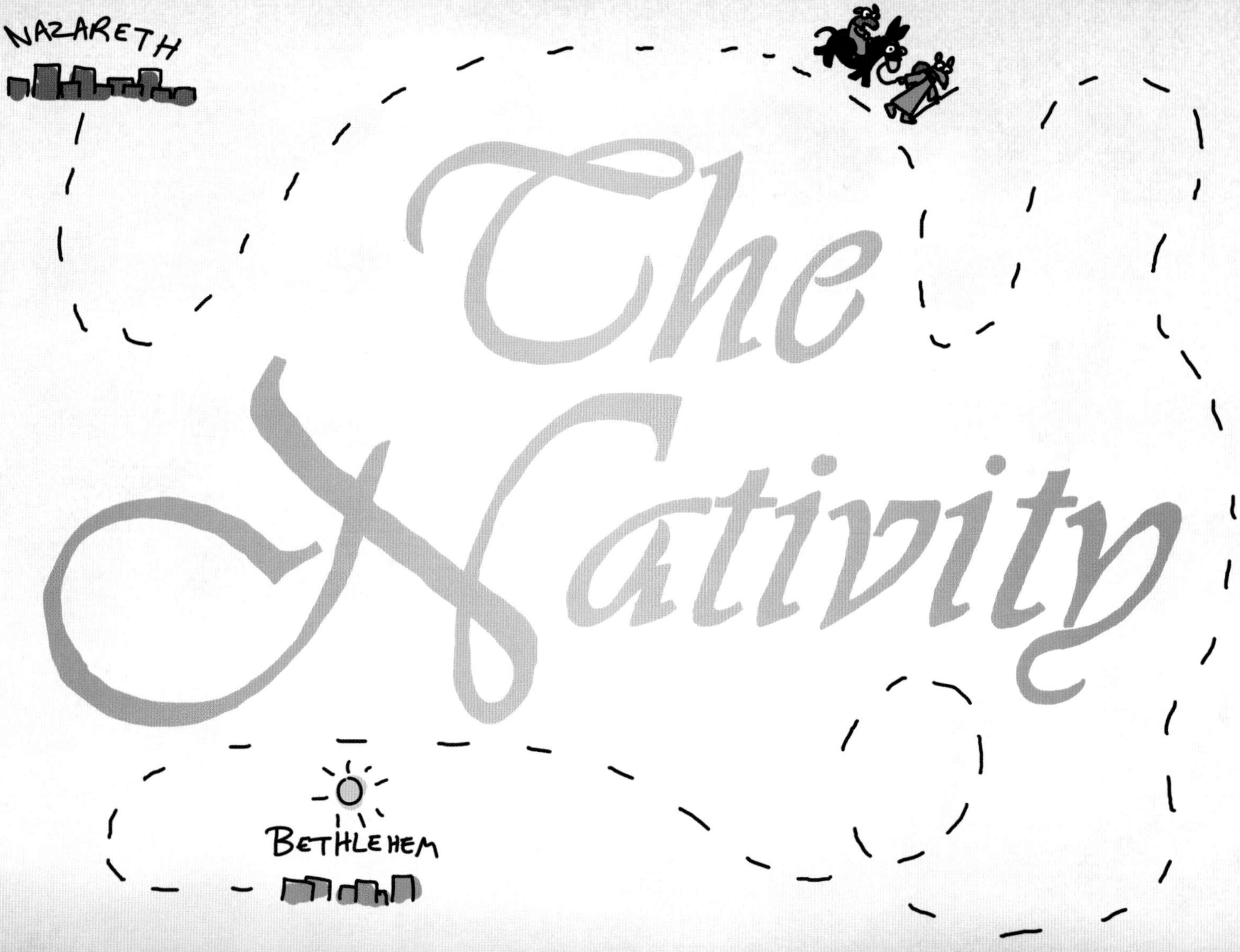
NAZARETH
BETHLEHEM

To Bethlehem, to Bethlehem!

But listen, my little pinch of belly-button lint, it was a long way to Bethlehem. It would have taken:

Four days if they walked (maybe a week if they walked slowly because Mary was pregnant)...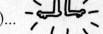

A day and a half if they both had a horse...

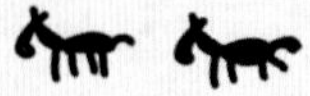

Twenty minutes if they had a rocket but rockets weren't invented yet.

If they had a *teleportation* robot they could have got there instantaneously but they weren't invented yet either and still haven't been which is an oversight if you ask me.

Perhaps they took a rowboat. Perhaps they took a donkey.

Luke doesn't say, so *we just don't know.*

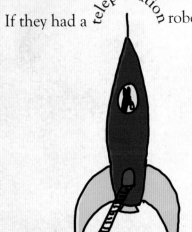

Excellent Space
Rocketty
Sort Of Thing
(Not invented then)

Teleportation Robot
(Not invented
at all)

Hey wait
a minute!

Teleportation Rowboat

24

One thing we do know is...

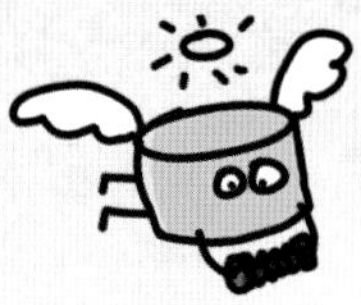
Angel cheese
with
accordion

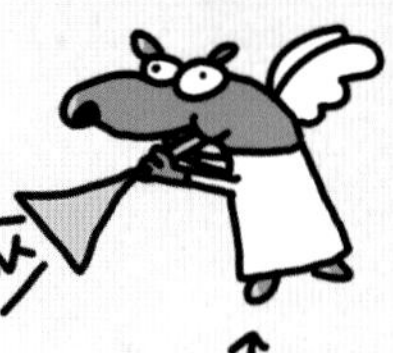
HONK
Angel
with
honker

There is no donkey in the Christmas story

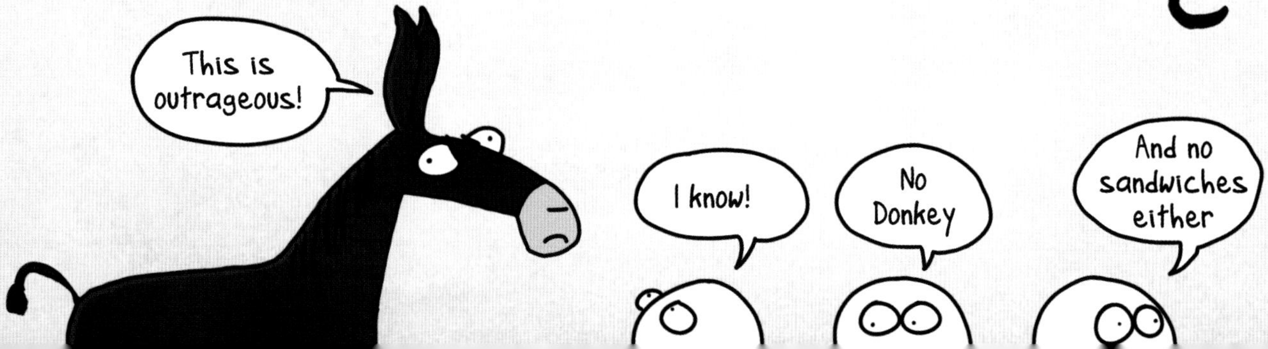
This is outrageous!
I know!
No Donkey
And no sandwiches either

No donkey?

But *everyone* had a beard and a donkey in those days, surely? Even some of the children.

There is ALWAYS a donkey in the Christmas Story. Isn't there?

I prefer to think of it as a currently under-utilised donkey vacancy.

Not according to Luke.

And when we asked Matthew?

I agree with whatever ol' beardy over there just said

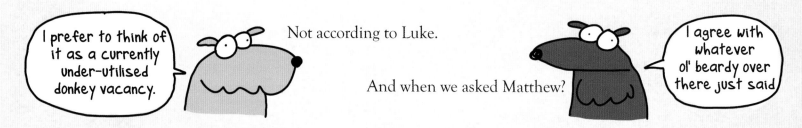

But there is ALWAYS a donkey – a brave and courageous donkey – in the Christmas Story.
There are loads of animals in **The Bible**, birds, oxes,
lions and everything else, but the donkey is the most Bibley animal of all.
They're everywhere!

I think perhaps you mean "Oxen"

So we shall have a donkey in our story, because they are splendid,
sturdy creatures. And because we can.

Now then, my little weasel trapped in a porridge pot, everyone knows the next bit of the story. Mary and Joseph and the donkey finally get to Bethlehem, only to find that all the accommodation is booked out.

Noooooo!

NO ROOM AT THE INN!

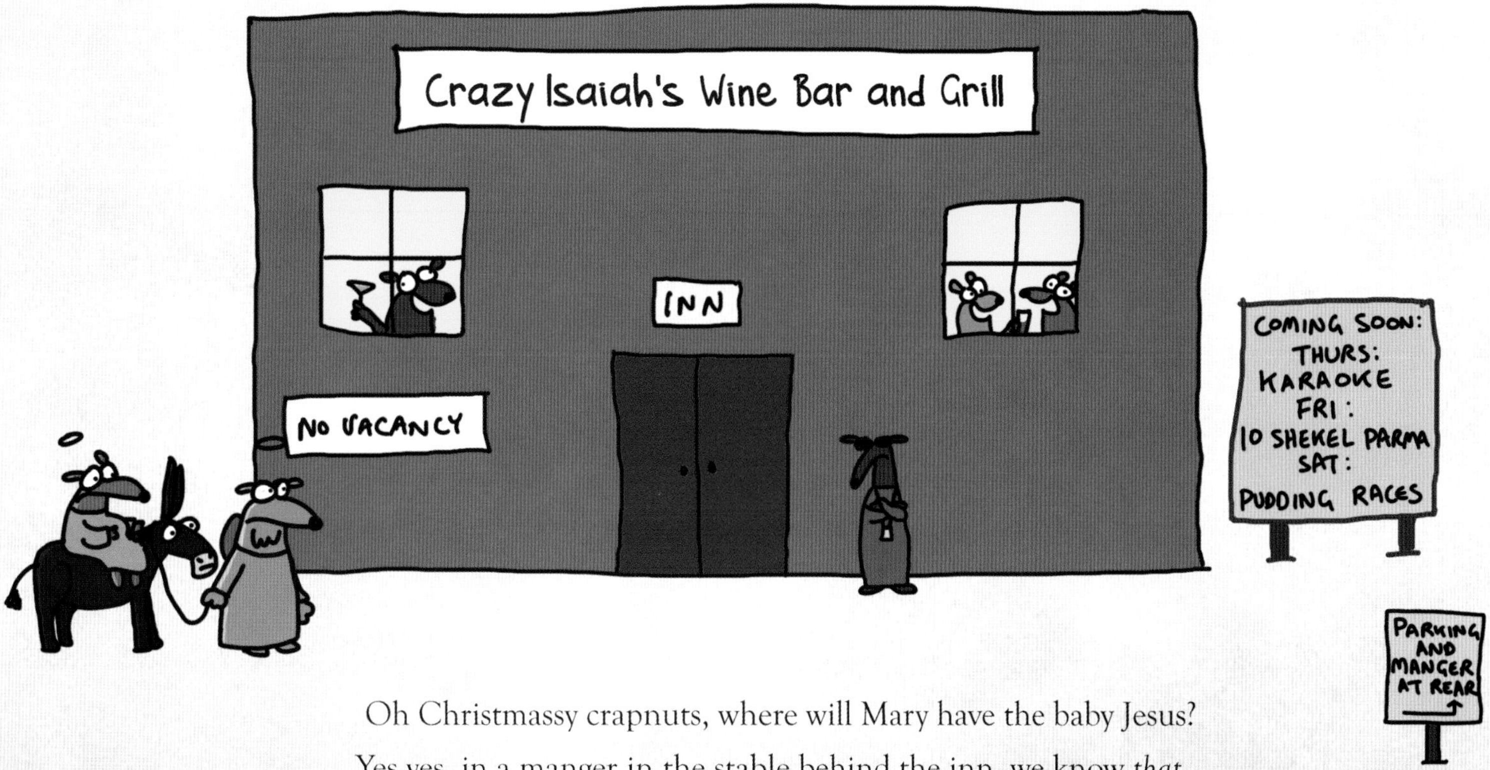
Crazy Isaiah's Wine Bar and Grill
INN
NO VACANCY
COMING SOON:
THURS:
KARAOKE
FRI:
10 SHEKEL PARMA
SAT:
PUDDING RACES
PARKING AND MANGER AT REAR

Oh Christmassy crapnuts, where will Mary have the baby Jesus?

Yes yes, in a manger in the stable behind the inn, we know *that*...

...But wait!

Because, my fluffy little rabbit's bottom, we're not even sure it was an inn, let alone a stable behind an inn. True! When Luke wrote this part he used the Greek word 'kataluma'. And kataluma does mean 'inn' but it also means 'spare room'.

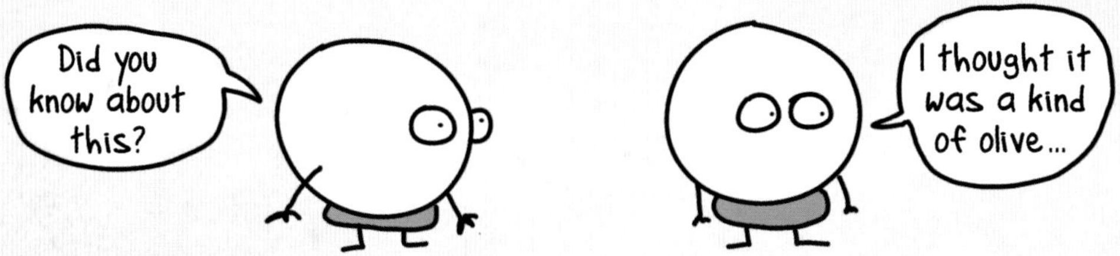
Did you know about this?
I thought it was a kind of olive...

Luke might have meant that they went to stay with Joseph's mum and dad, only to find that Joseph's gran was already quite comfortably set up in the spare room, thank you very much.

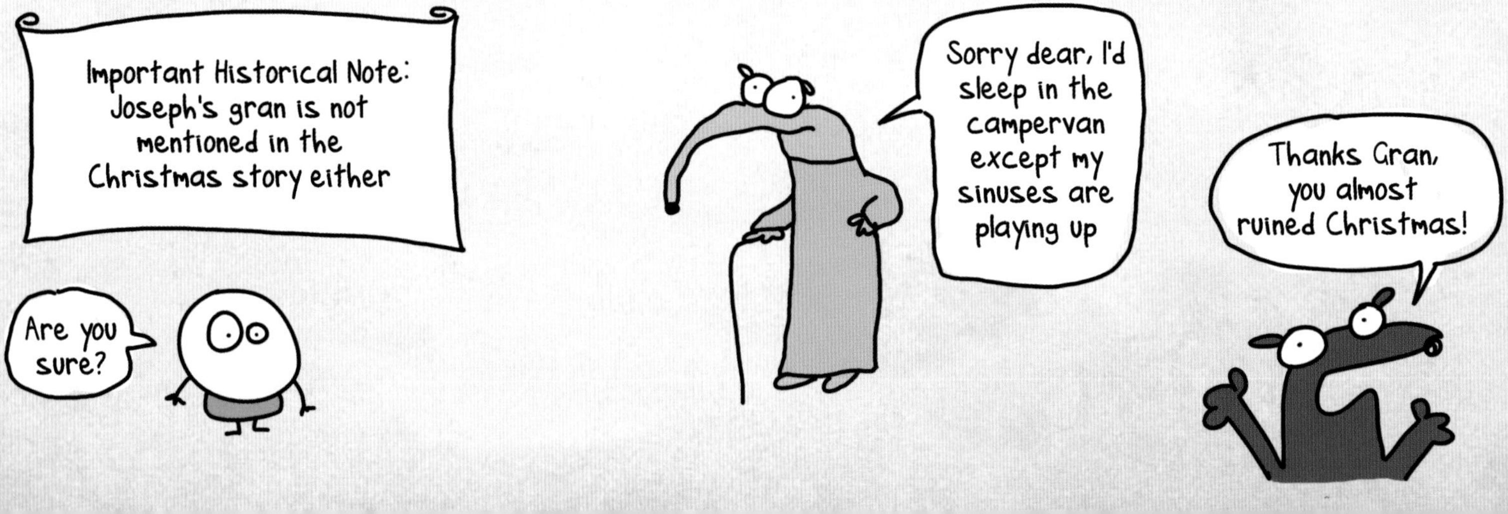
Important Historical Note: Joseph's gran is not mentioned in the Christmas story either
Are you sure?
Sorry dear, I'd sleep in the campervan except my sinuses are playing up
Thanks Gran, you almost ruined Christmas!

Well, where did they stay then?

In times past, my fragrant little pile of donkey poop, lots of people kept their sheep and oxens* indoors, on the ground floor of the house itself. You could have had a sheep in the downstairs lounge room with the chickens.

Mangers weren't just found in stables – they could be anywhere!

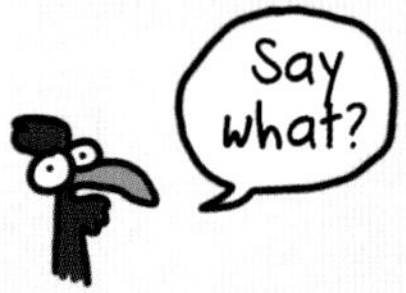
Say what?

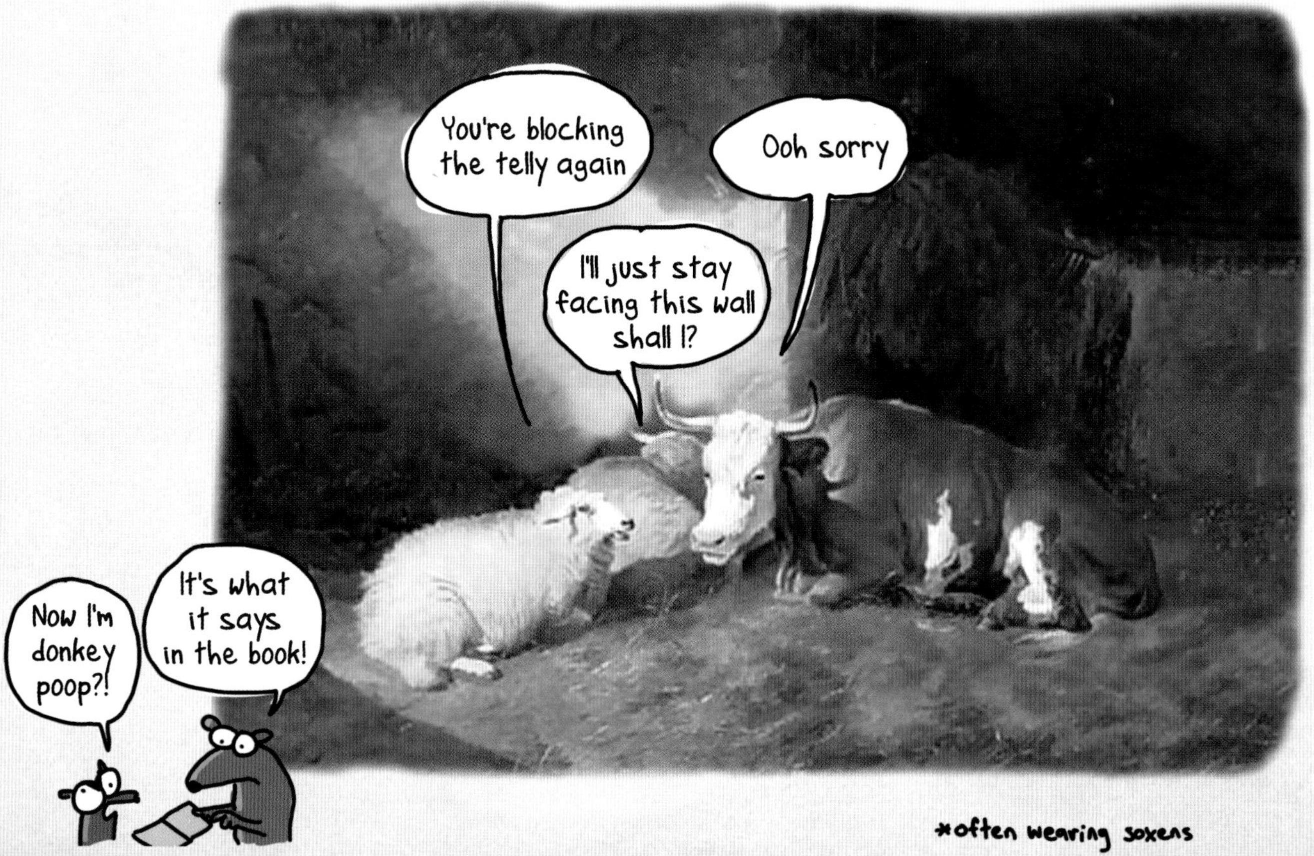
You're blocking the telly again
Ooh sorry
I'll just stay facing this wall shall I?
Now I'm donkey poop?!
It's what it says in the book!

*often wearing soxens

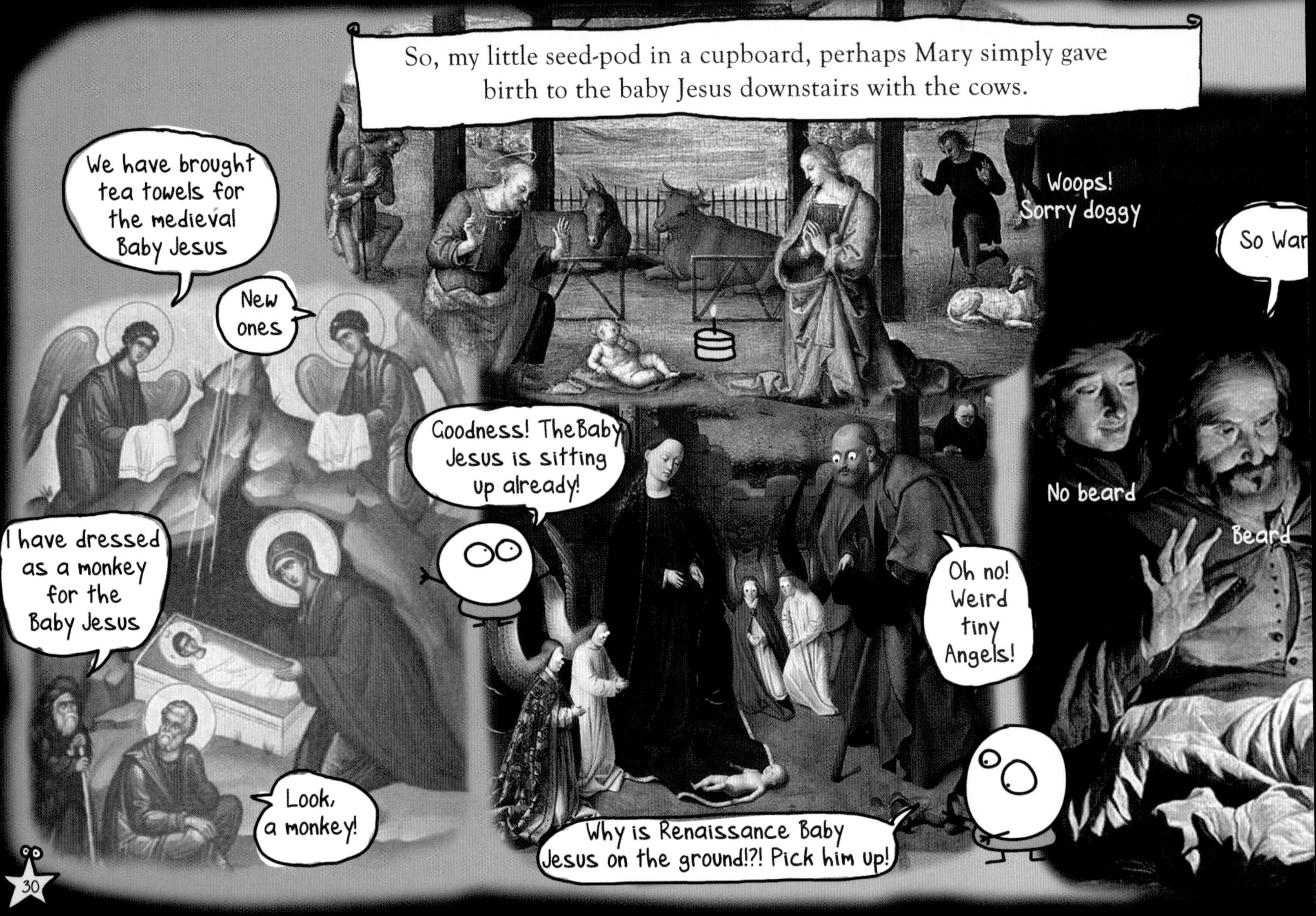
So, my little seed-pod in a cupboard, perhaps Mary simply gave birth to the baby Jesus downstairs with the cows.
We have brought tea towels for the medieval Baby Jesus
New ones
I have dressed as a monkey for the Baby Jesus
Look, a monkey!
Goodness! The Baby Jesus is sitting up already!
Oh no! Weird tiny Angels!
Why is Renaissance Baby Jesus on the ground!?! Pick him up!
Woops! Sorry doggy
So War
No beard
Beard

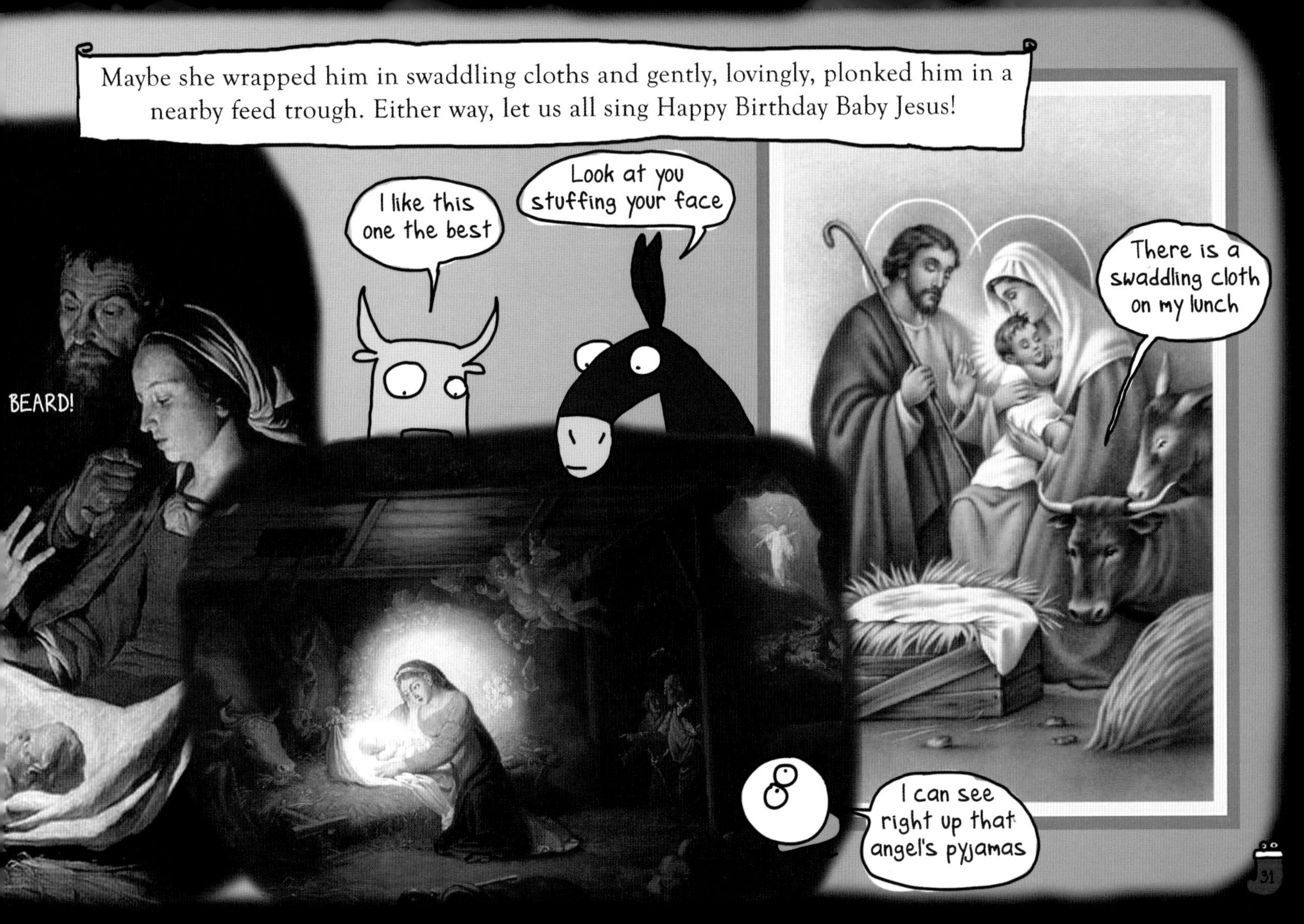
Maybe she wrapped him in swaddling cloths and gently, lovingly, plonked him in a nearby feed trough. Either way, let us all sing Happy Birthday Baby Jesus!
BEARD!
I like this one the best
Look at you stuffing your face
There is a swaddling cloth on my lunch
I can see right up that angel's pyjamas

More Excitementy Yuletide Facts – Christmas Trees – The Truth!

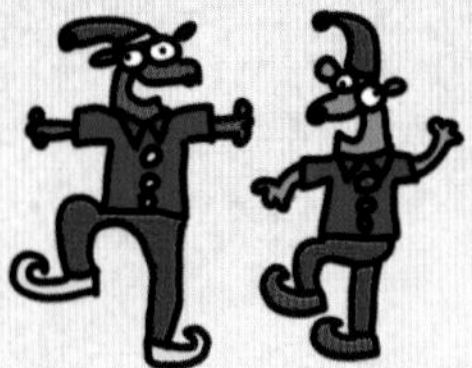

a pair of wood spirits with their stupid shoes

Did you know – Pagan families would bring a live tree into the house as a place for wood spirits to keep warm in winter

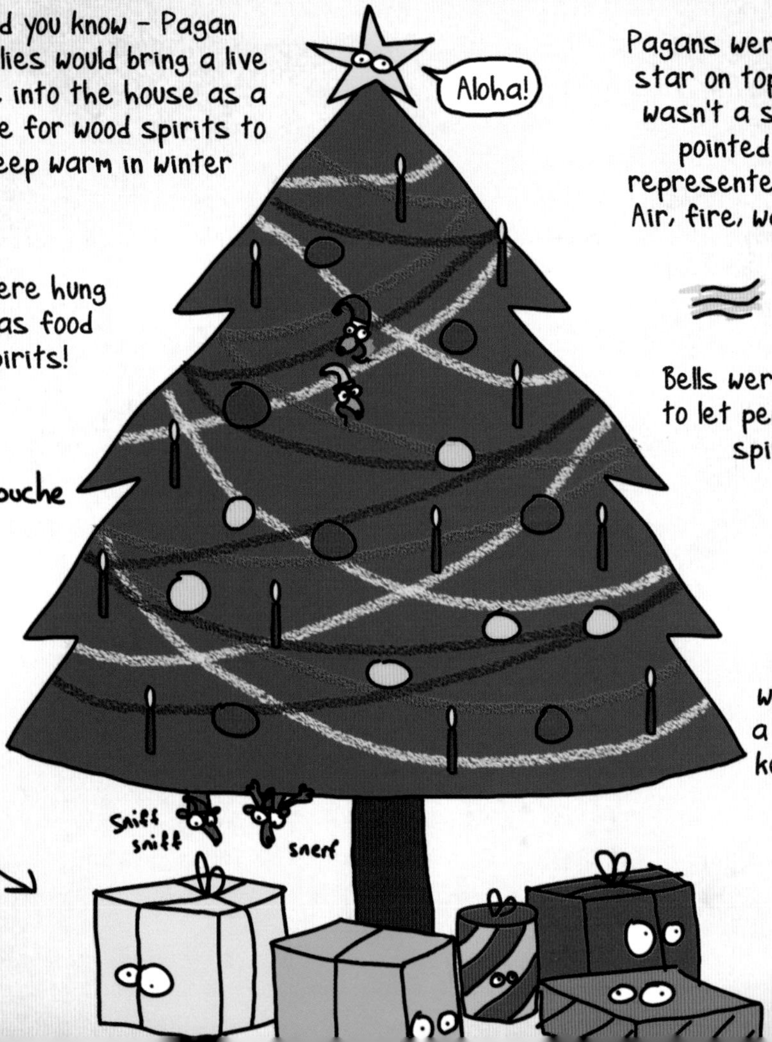

Aloha!
sniff sniff
snerf

Pagans were the first to put a star on top of the tree, but it wasn't a star, it was a five-pointed pentagram that represented the five elements! Air, fire, water, earth, cheese

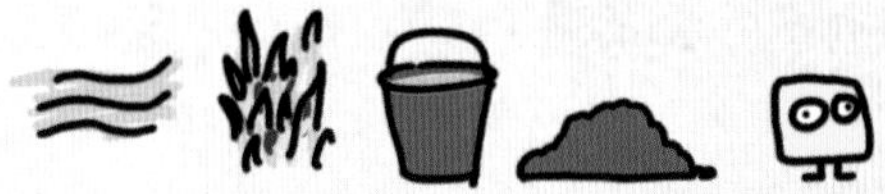

Food and treats were hung on the branches as food for the wood spirits!

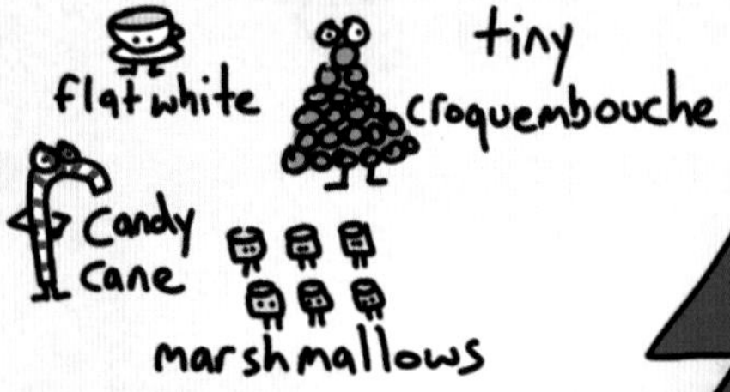

flat white
tiny croquembouche
candy cane
marshmallows

Bells were hung on the branches to let people know when the wood spirits were present

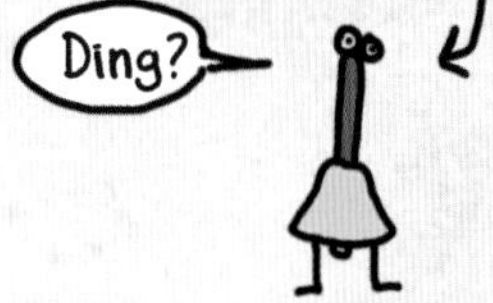

Ding?

Christmas tree lights were originally designed as a sort of electric fence to keep children and livestock away from the presents

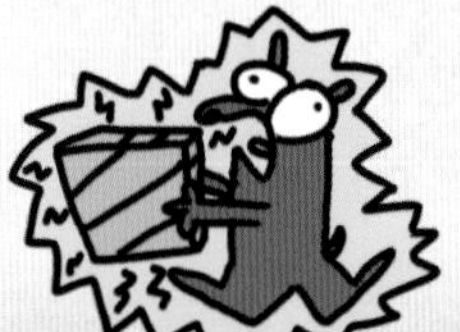

Presents were originally a Roman custom and they used special wrapping paper knitted from guinea pig poo. True!*

*This is not true

The Shepherds

Meanwhile, just outside Bethlehem,
a group of shepherds were out in the fields
shepherding their sheep, when an angel appeared to tell
them about the baby Jesus.

Do not be afraid for behold I bring you good tidings of great joy. It's a boy! And everyone is doing just fine.

As if one angel is not enough excitement for the night, a whole choir of angels springs up and they sing

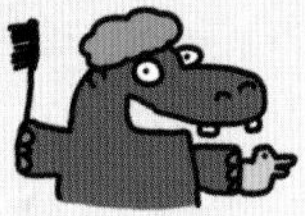

Hippo Bath Day Baby Jesus and just as quickly nip off back to Heaven again.

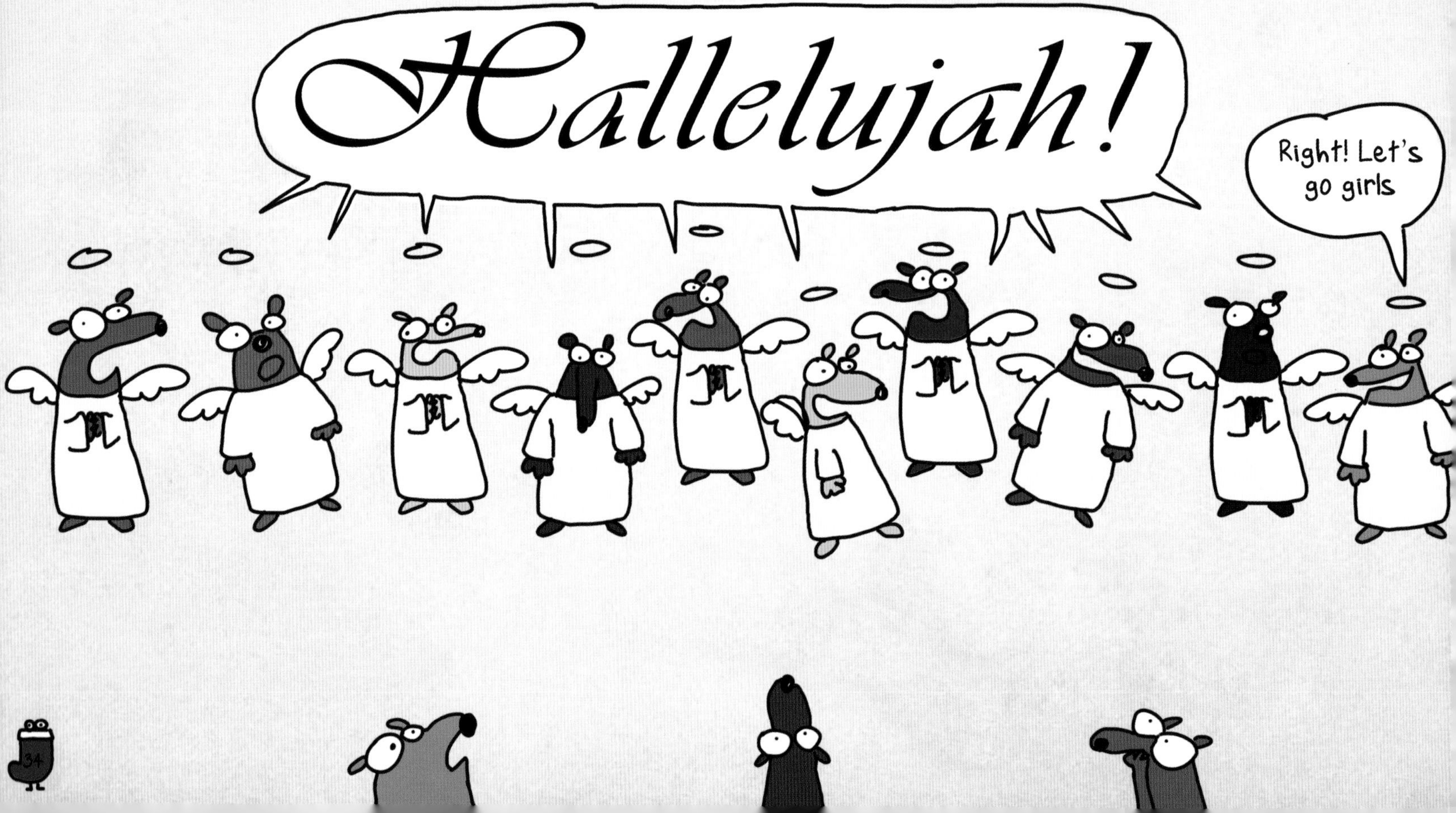
Hallelujah!
Right! Let's go girls

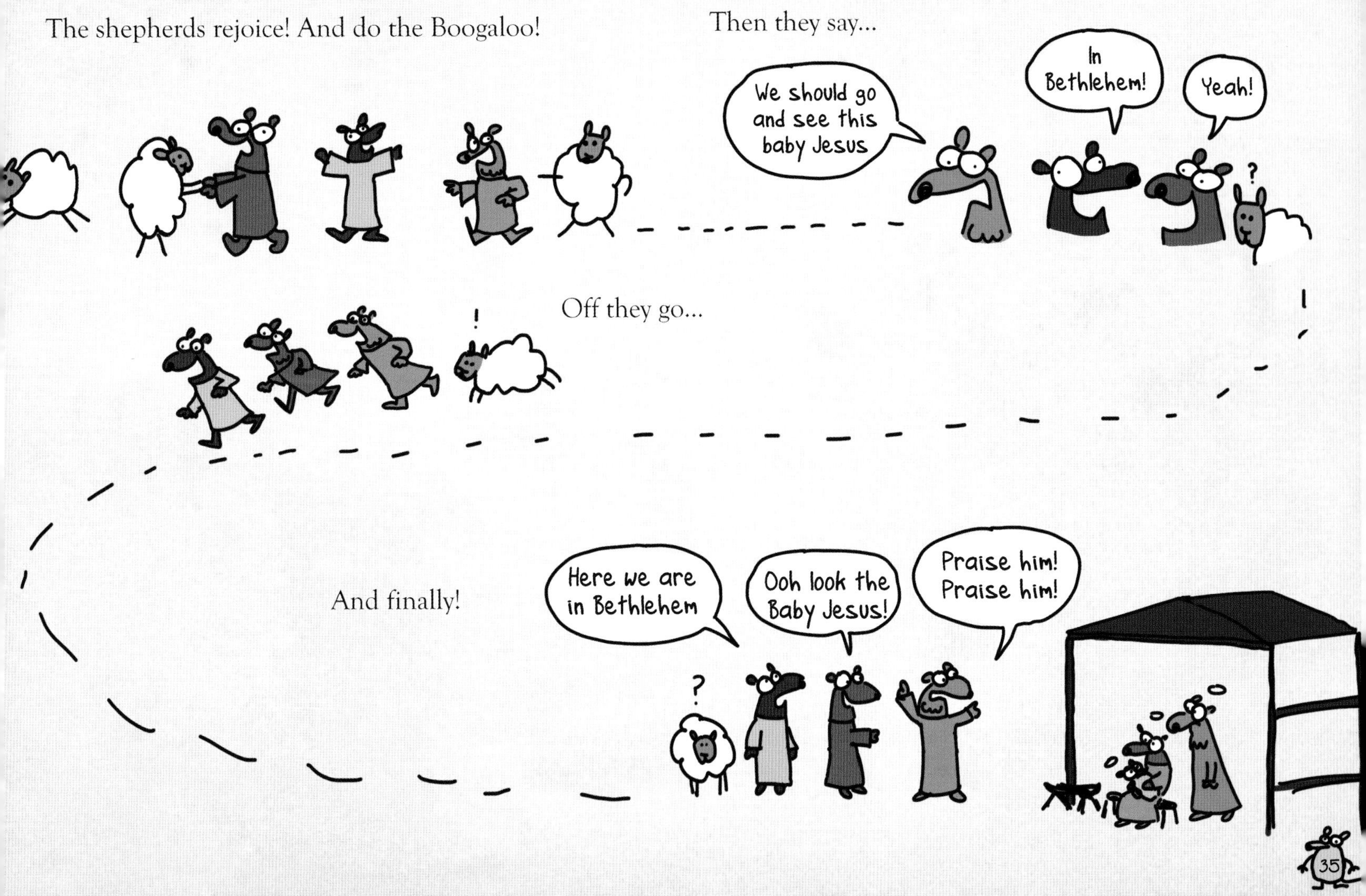
The shepherds rejoice! And do the Boogaloo!
Then they say...
We should go and see this baby Jesus
In Bethlehem!
Yeah!
?
Off they go...
!
And finally!
Here we are in Bethlehem
Ooh look the Baby Jesus!
Praise him! Praise him!
?

But just a minute, my delicious weihnachtsplätzchen, Luke doesn't say what the shepherds did with their sheep.

What? I beg your pudding?

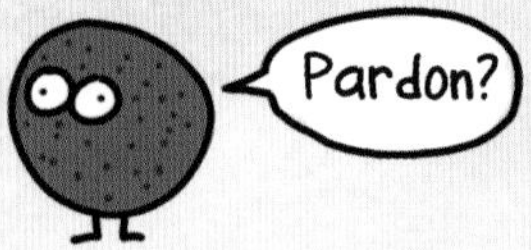
Pardon?

Did they take them all to visit the baby Jesus in the loungeroom with the cow? How would they all fit? Did they leave them behind with someone who had to miss out on seeing the baby Jesus at Christmas?

Maybe they put them on THE SHEEP BUS!

BAAAAAAAAP BAAAAAP LOOOK OUUUT!!!

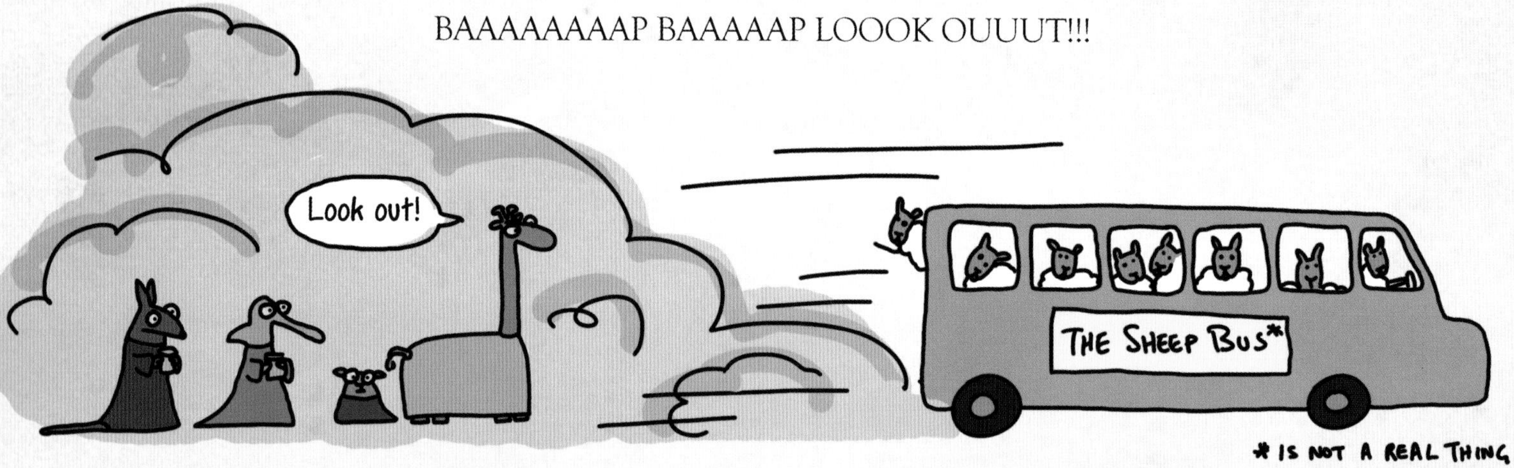
Look out!
THE SHEEP BUS*
* IS NOT A REAL THING

And maybe they didn't because they didn't have a bus and sheep can't drive that is just silly.

Adoration of the Magii

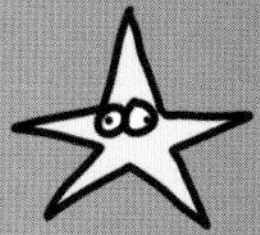

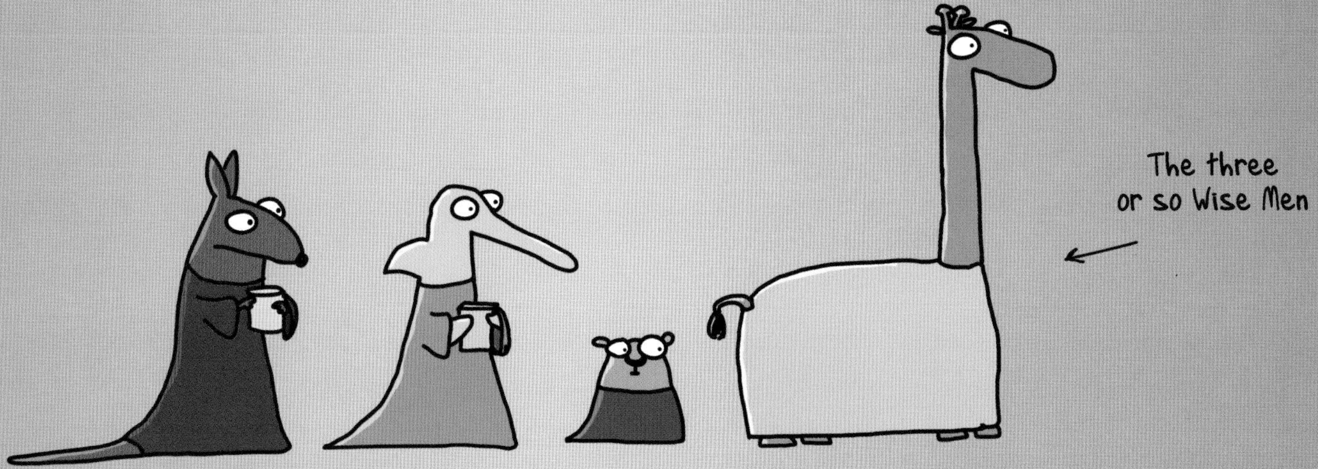
The three
or so Wise Men

Meanwhile, my most precious titanium shoe-horn, back at **The Gospel of Matthew...**

Not long after Jesus was born some wise men from the east came to Jerusalem.

Matthew doesn't say how many there were, he just says they went to see King Herod.

'We are here to worship the new king please,' they said. What lovely manners!

INFORMATION
welcome
Excuse me, we're looking for the Baby Jesus
We're from the East
Aloha
We followed the star

New king? hmmmm
King Herod is up to no good!
BETHLEHEM

King Herod pointed them in the direction of Bethlehem and off they went, the however-many-there-were wise men following the Star in the East as their guide.

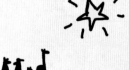

This is the first mention of the Star in the East. True!

Some people put a star on top of their Christmas tree, other people put an Angel

I prefer a star. The pine needles scratch my bottom
Angel Bottom

The wise men were just as excited as the shepherds to arrive at the manger because look! It's the baby Jesus! They fell to their knees and worshipped him. And then, my dearest slice of individually wrapped cheese, the wise men presented the baby Jesus with:

Gold, Frankincense and Myrrh.

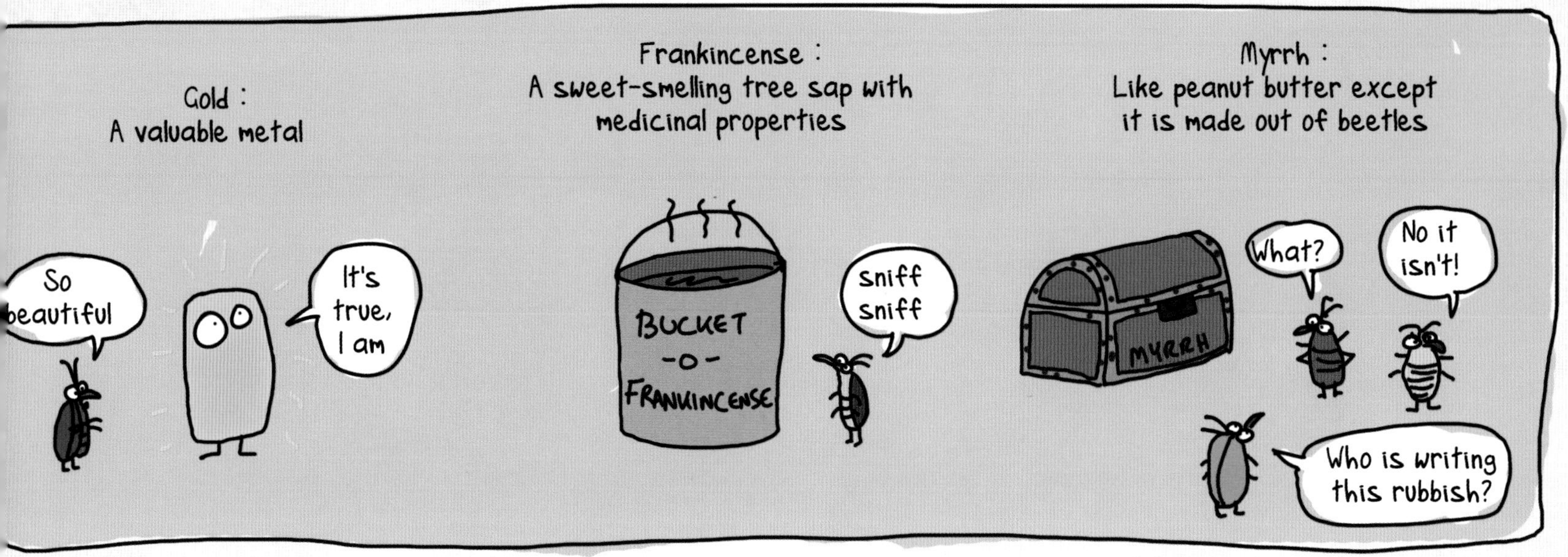
Gold : A valuable metal
Frankincense : A sweet-smelling tree sap with medicinal properties
Myrrh : Like peanut butter except it is made out of beetles
So beautiful
It's true, I am
BUCKET -O- FRANKINCENSE
sniff sniff
MYRRH
What?
No it isn't!
Who is writing this rubbish?

Maybe, my snap-frozen poffertje, everyone decided that because there were three presents, there must have been three wise men. Matthew is silent on the subject. But three is a good number to fit in a nativity scene so why not? And anyway, Christmas presents!

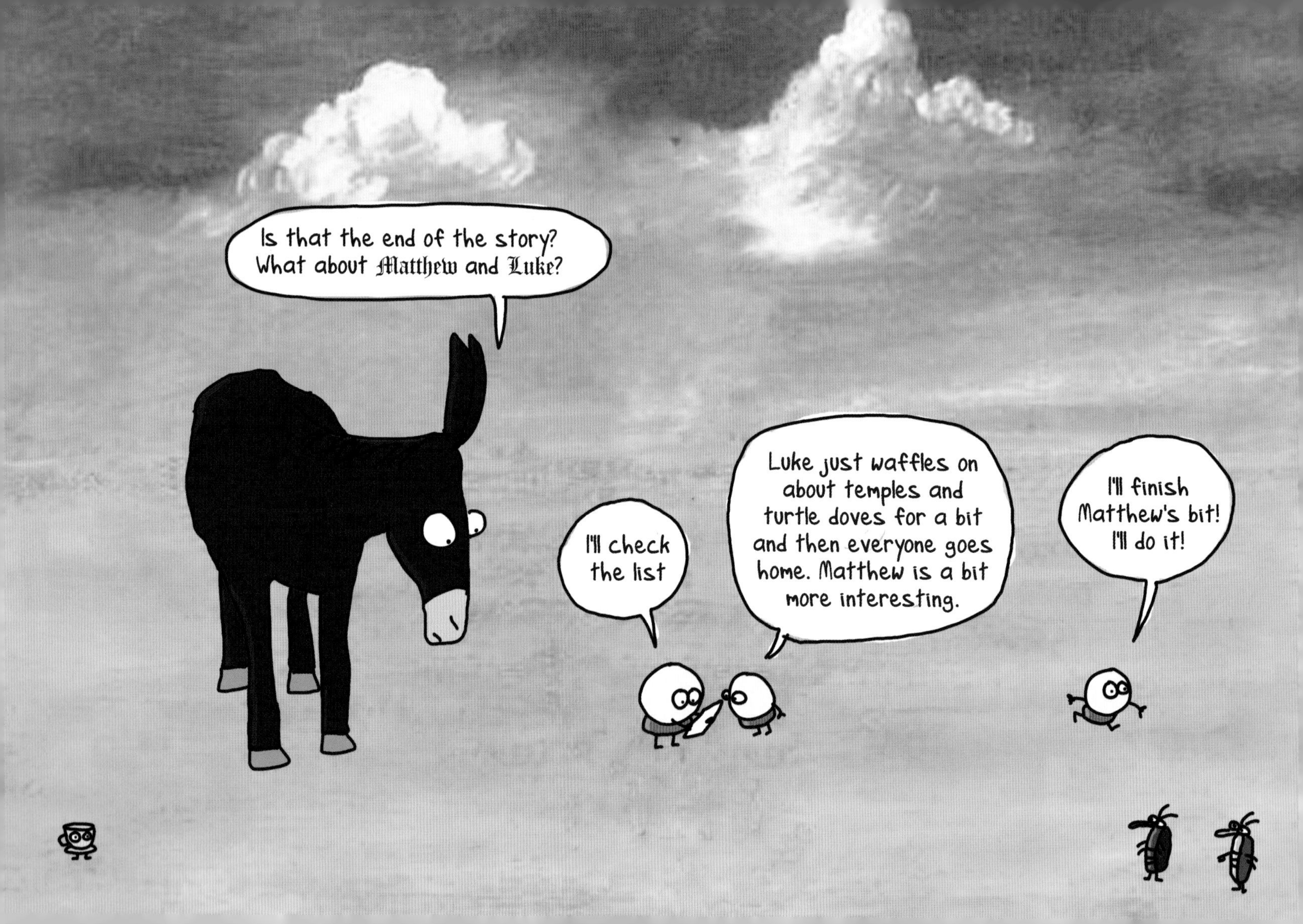
Is that the end of the story? What about Matthew and Luke?
I'll check the list
Luke just waffles on about temples and turtle doves for a bit and then everyone goes home. Matthew is a bit more interesting.
I'll finish Matthew's bit! I'll do it!

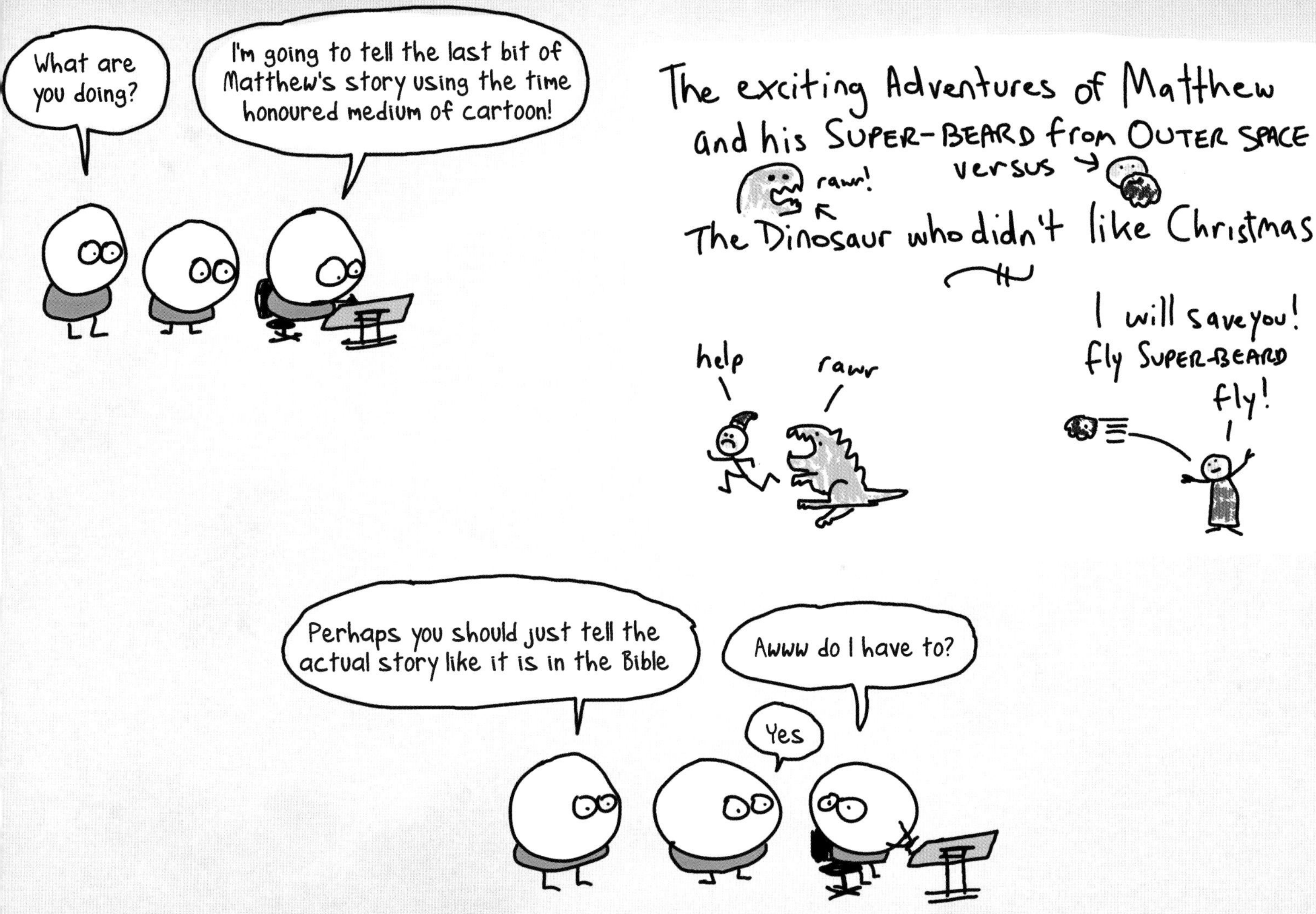
What are you doing?
I'm going to tell the last bit of Matthew's story using the time honoured medium of cartoon!
The exciting Adventures of Matthew and his SUPER-BEARD from OUTER SPACE versus The Dinosaur who didn't like Christmas
rawr!
help
rawr
I will save you! fly SUPER-BEARD fly!
Perhaps you should just tell the actual story like it is in the Bible
Awww do I have to?
Yes

the end of the story by A. Scallop

When the Wise men came
what really happened was that
Herod was jealous of Jesus →

Jesus!

haha

So he sent the Wise men to
spy on Jesus for him

~~then a dinosaur ate him~~

no it didn't

But the Wise Men didn't
know Herod was bad until
an Angel told them

Herod is really really bad

Then they ran off home back East

~~and a dinosaur ate them~~

no!

and Herod was so angry

~~he turned into a dinosaur~~

no!

rawr

Herod planned to do terrible
things so an Angel warned Joseph

run away!

And they ran away to Egypt

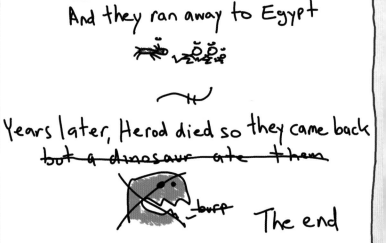

Years later, Herod died so they came back

~~but a dinosaur ate them~~

~~burp~~

The end

The Further Truth about Christmas – the final part in a series of ever so many!

Tinsel was invented in Germany in 1913 by Klaus Von Tinselhoeffer to entertain Robert, his giant squid. Klaus was often away from home, so Robert would become lonely and try to eat the neighbours. Unfortunately Robert had no interest in tinsel, which nonetheless went on to become the charming Christmas decoration we know today.

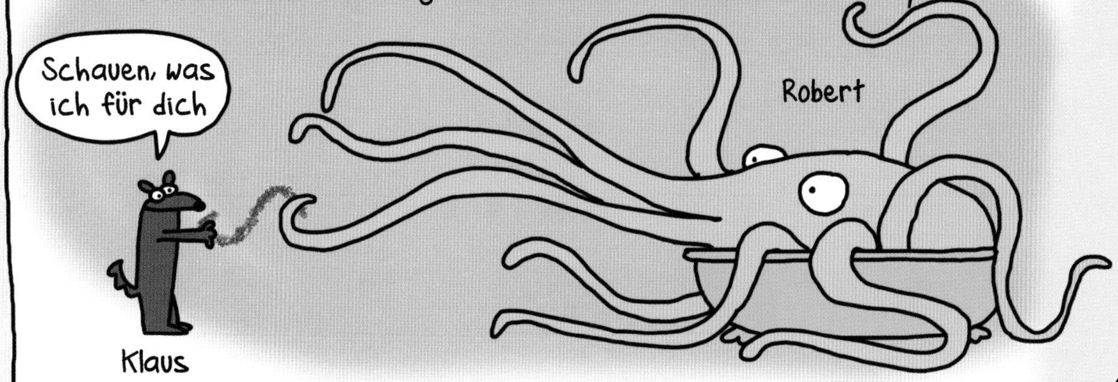
Schauen, was ich für dich
Robert
Klaus

In 1223, St Francis of Assisi created the first nativity scene in Greccio, Italy, using live mice and a roast chicken. Today's nativity scenes can include pretty much anything because it's Christmas and everyone is welcome!

"While shepherds watched their flocks by night"
Did you know shepherds didn't watch at night in winter, only in the spring, when the lambs were newborn? Jesus was probably born in spring in 2 BC (Before Christ). So Jesus was born 2 years before he was born and so when he was born he was 2? Oh my goodness!

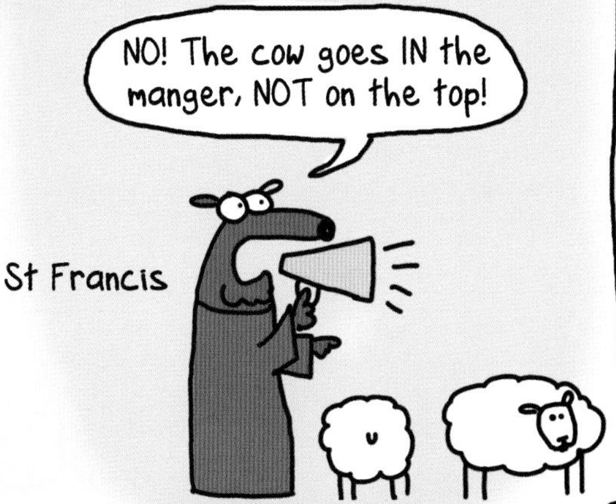
NO! The cow goes IN the manger, NOT on the top!
St Francis

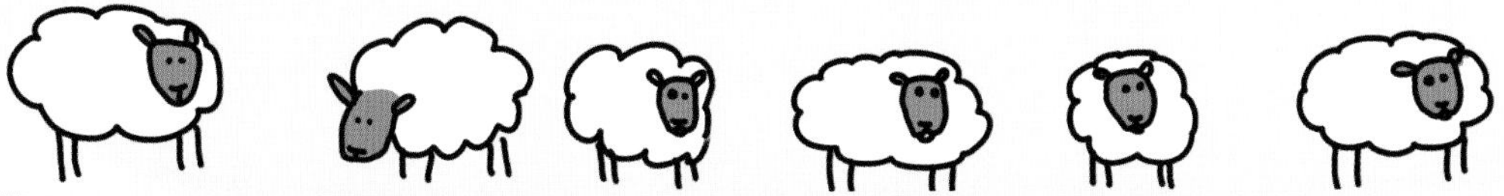

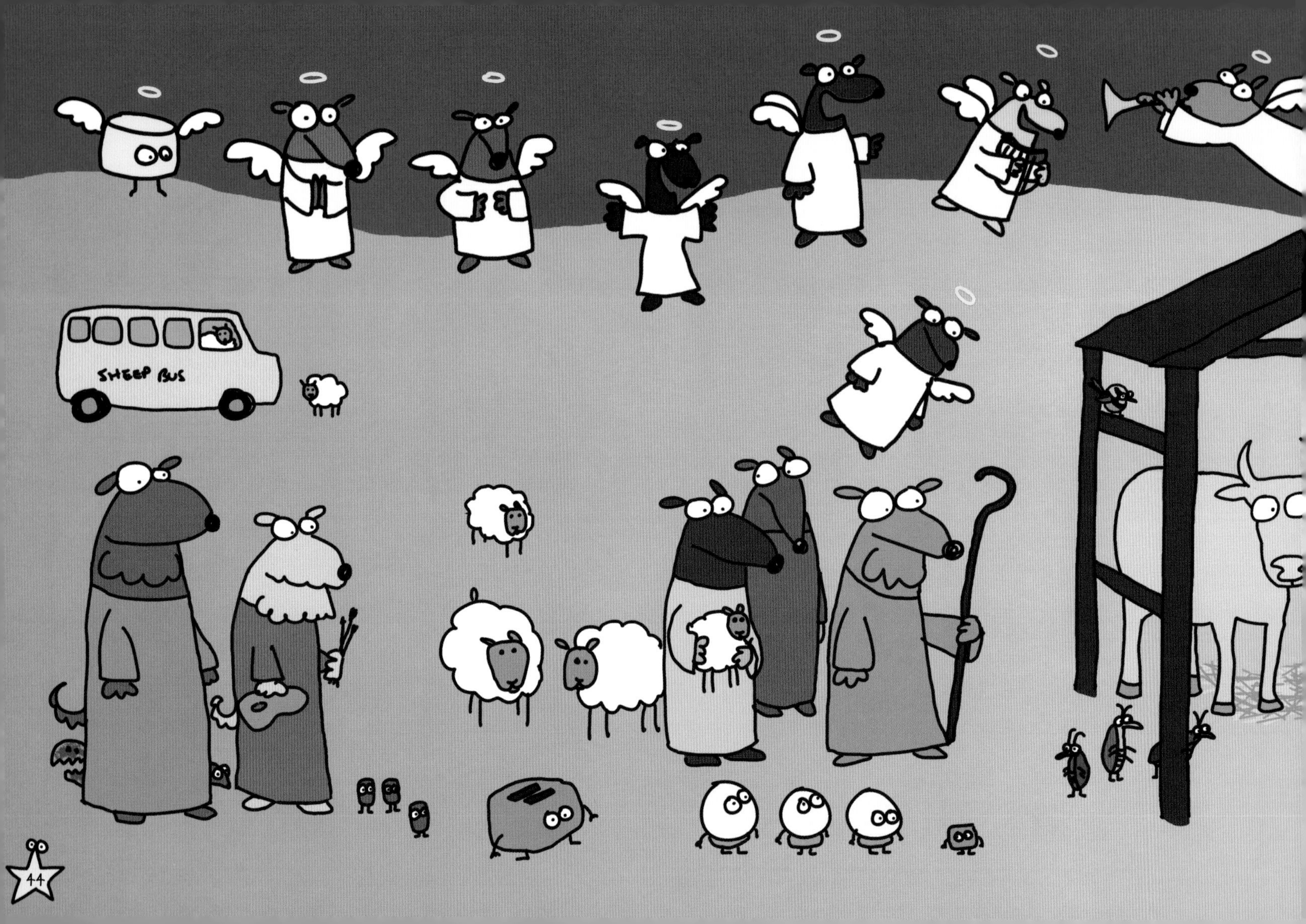
SHEEP BUS

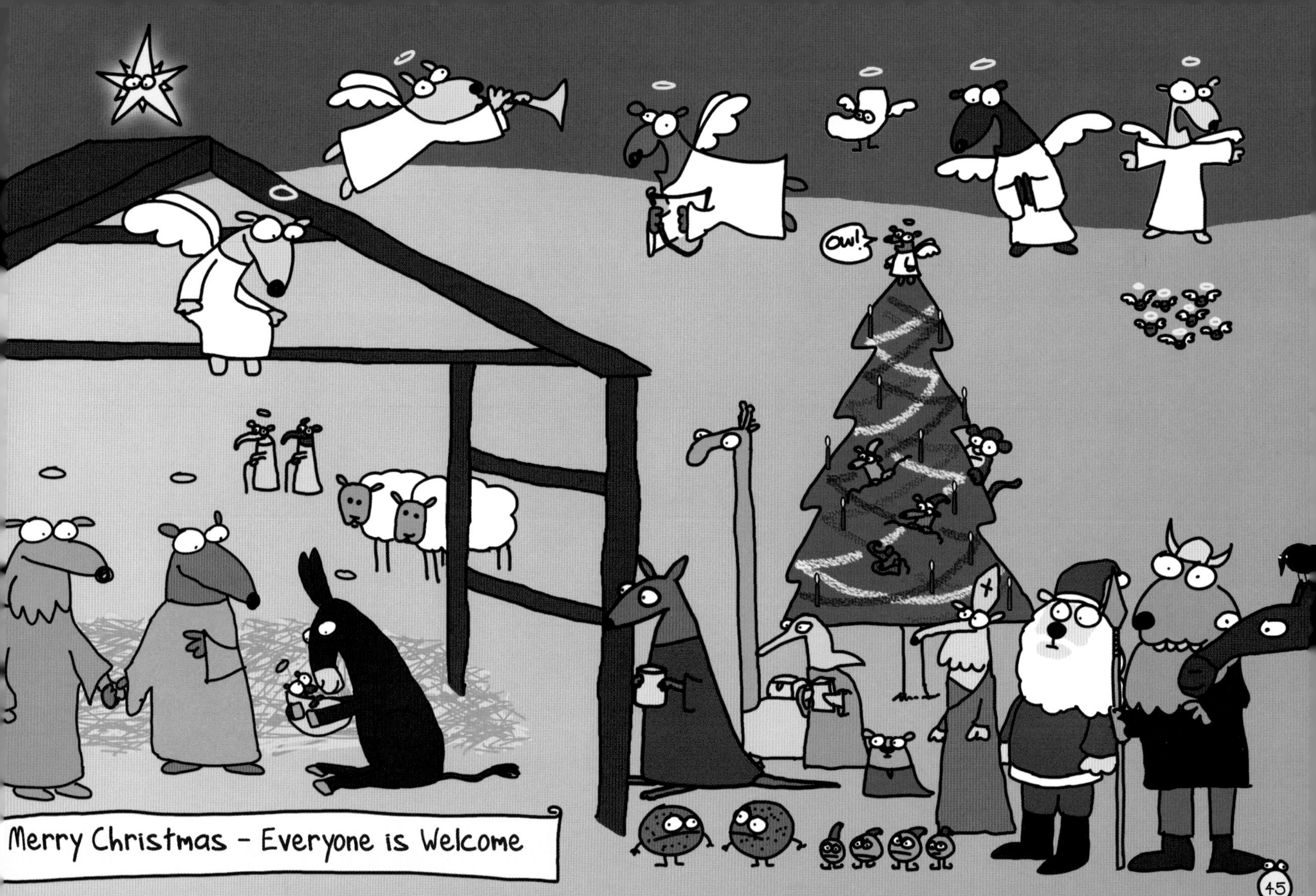
Ow!
Merry Christmas - Everyone is Welcome

So my beloved Christmas tree bauble, this really is the end of the Christmas Story,
and our story of the Christmas Story.
Whether or not they went to Egypt, however they got there and got back, and perhaps they
never even left, Jesus and his parents ended up living in Nazareth
with the donkey.
Or at least I say they did.

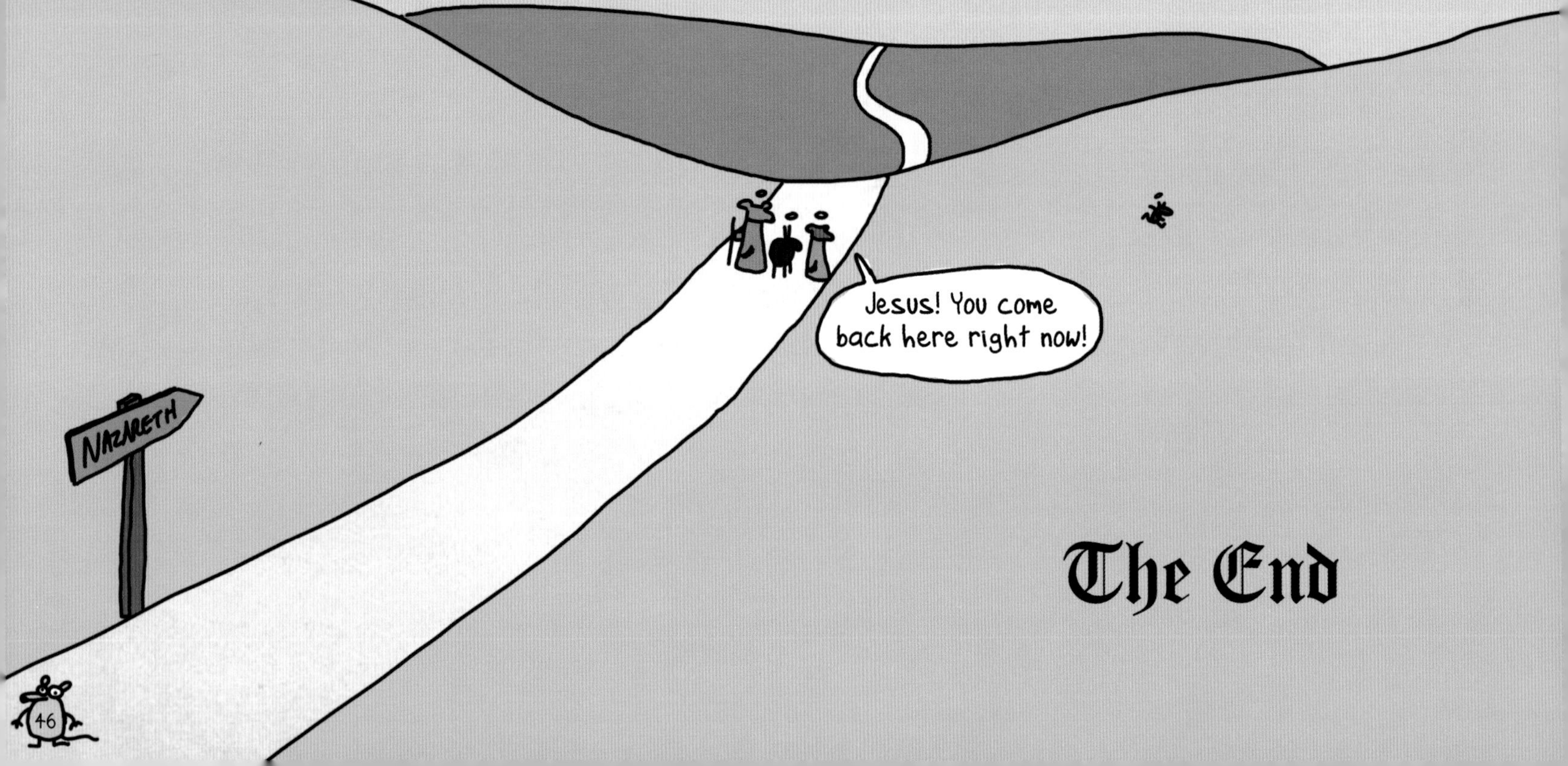

Jesus! You come back here right now!
NAZARETH

The End

Thanks to Zoë, Ruby, Mandy, Sophie, Peanut, Chong, Chu Chu, Di, the
Frog, the two Ambers, Jade, Leigh, Guy, Mr Crook, JJ, Anastasia and
anyone who ever looked under a tree.
All research was done as shonkily as possible mostly via the internet
and a free copy of the Bible I got one time.

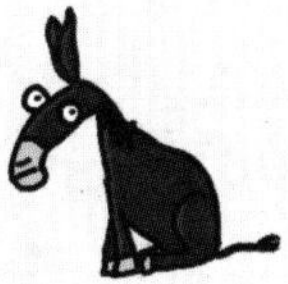